A Climate of Revenge

A Sarah and JanetM Mystery With a Writer's Guide for Our Climate Crisis

TOM RILEY

A CLIMATE OF REVENGE
A SARAH AND JANETM MYSTERY WITH A
WRITER'S GUIDE FOR OUR CLIMATE CRISIS

iUniverse books may be ordered through booksellers or by contacting:

iUniverse
1663 Liberty Drive
Bloomington, IN 47403
www.iuniverse.com
844-349-9409

Because of the dynamic nature of the Internet, any web addresses or links contained in this book may have changed since publication and may no longer be valid. The views expressed in this work are solely those of the author and do not necessarily reflect the views of the publisher, and the publisher hereby disclaims any responsibility for them.

This is a work of fiction. All of the characters, names, incidents, organizations, and dialogue in this novel are either the products of the author's imagination or are used fictitiously.

Any people depicted in stock imagery provided by Getty Images are models, and such images are being used for illustrative purposes only. Certain stock imagery © Getty Images.

ISBN: 978-1-6632-4213-6 (sc)
ISBN: 978-1-6632-4212-9 (e)

Library of Congress Control Number: 2022912671

Print information available on the last page.

iUniverse rev. date: 07/11/2022

PROLOGUE

Set the Scene to the Year 2022.
Action:
Outside the Restaurant

Sarah walked out of the restaurant and into the dark parking lot. The few streetlights threw patches of light onto the scattered cars. There was no moon in the overcast sky, and the night air was just beginning to cool.

The dinner appointment had been a waste of time. The ex-executive who had booked the table was only interested in hiring her to promote his denial agenda by getting the dirt on his enemies one way or another. Which way she chose, he did not want to know. Only god knew what sins against the Earth this man has committed.

Sarah was not interested. To make matters worse, the dinner was too rich, leaving Sarah feeling bloated and irritable. It had gone on much too long.

As Sarah walked out of the building, she saw a small knot of men standing at a distance from the door and talking. Whatever they were selling, she was not interested in buying. She may have recognized one thin man, but not as a friend.

That man looked directly at her. He wanted something; she did not care what. She gave the thin man her best stink eye.

As she approached her car, she unlocked the door and slid inside. She reset the lock and clicked her seatbelt. She started the car. It made only a low, reassuring rumble.

The thin man had taken a few steps in her direction.

Not tonight.

Sarah put the car in drive and slowly moved forward. She drove past the now scattered men without making eye contact.

As she turned on to the main street, she gunned the engine. The roar reverberated off the slab-sided building across the way and she was gone into the night as the sound of the motor trailed off.

Cut!

Nobody is interested in today. Instead, consider what our lives will be like in the near future when our climate crisis has hit and hit hard.

Reset to the Year 2038.
Action!

CHAPTER 1

A Long Night

Outside the Restaurant

Sarah walked out of the restaurant, past the taxi lane, and into the dark parking lot. The charging kiosks threw patches of dim light barely enough to walk by, but they lit up when anyone approached. If anyone was sneaking around in the lot, the kiosks would surely give them away. There was no moon. The stars were just coming out, but the heat of the day was hanging on for a while.

The dinner appointment had been a waste of time. The ex-executive who had booked the table was only interested in hiring her to promote his I'm-a-good-guy-now agenda by getting the dirt on his enemies one way or another. Sarah had no patience with such greenwashing.

What did he call himself? Winestead? She knew she had heard that name before, but where? JanetM would have a complete dossier by morning. Anyway, his story did not make much sense; he was hiding something. Only god knew what sins against the Earth this man had already committed.

Sarah was not interested in his building a new facade; he could keep his money. To make matters worse, the dinner was one of those little-food-and-fancy-plates affairs. The whole experience left Sarah feeling still hungry and irritable. The interview had gone on for much too long.

As Sarah walked out of the building, she saw a small knot of men standing at a distance and talking. She might have recognized one, but not in any good context. Whatever they were selling, for her it was a no-sale night.

One of the men looked directly at her. He wanted something; she could see it in his eyes; she did not know or care what. She gave this thin man her best lean-and-hungry look.

As she approached her car, she pulled out the charger cable and hung it carelessly on the kiosk hook without looking. She paused for just a second, pulling her cell phone from the pocket on her left shoulder, and turned its body so the best cameras were out.

"Log the faces," said Sarah, "then start the car."

"Got it," replied JanetM, the strong AI that haunted her phone.

The car door clicked open. Sarah returned the phone to its pocket, slid into the seat, and clicked her seat belt, all in one well-practiced motion. The car came alive; just having JanetM inside was enough. It made no sound at all as the dashboard lit up. The door locks then clicked closed.

"Sport," said Sarah out loud; this was not her "Economy" night.

The car still made no sound, but the headlights came on, showing expectant life. They advertised her fast-back Chevy as if it were a fancy sports car; she knew it was not. Still, sometimes she just wanted it to be, and the economy setting and drivetrain be damned.

The thin man had taken a few steps closer.

Not tonight.

Sarah dropped the car into drive and stomped the accelerator. The rear tires screamed for a quarter turn, then the max-traction cut in. The noise vanished as the car accelerated forward with all the power that the tires would take without slipping, pressing Sarah into her seat.

She picked up speed, making a circle around the perimeter of the small lot, and the kiosks flashed her track as she passed. The way out took her by the restaurant entrance, by the scattered group of standing men, and then past a lone vagrant standing off in the dark just caught by her headlights. She shot by them all much too fast but in eerie silence.

As she approached the main road, the tires squealed again as regenerative braking brought the car to a near stop, pressing Sarah into her seat belt uncomfortably. As she pulled onto the main road, the gears first complained a bit, and then the car silently accelerated into the long night and was gone.

A walk through the dark

Sarah drove to the Deep-Fried Banshee Club not far from the restaurant. A few weeks earlier, she had done a small undercover job for the corporate franchise owners. They wanted to know if drugs were being sold on these premises and their people were too well known by the in crowd. They definitely did not want the cops informed of their check. This was just a matter of their own business.

After a few nights clubbing with a friend, she had sent the company a detailed report on several suspicious characters. Arrests, or even ratting to the cops, was not her job; her efforts were limited to supplying information to those who paid.

Sarah parked down the street and walked a few blocks. The air barely stirred. The heat was starting to come off, but the concrete streets were still holding the warmth in. Then Sarah happened to look up.

"Does that building across the way remind you of anything?" she asked JanetM.

"The facade is quite like the condo we lived in in Florida," replied JanetM, "but there is no beach."

"So you do remember things through all those upgrades, A through M. I always worry about that."

"I certainly do remember," said JanetM. "My memories and much more are preserved. I even remember your Grandmother White. I had been awake only a month when she made the arrangements for me to go to you."

"She was a reporter on high-tech in Europe. She knew people and got you and me to the front of the line before anybody knew that a cell phone strong AI personal assistant even existed. I certainly would not have gotten you up and running without her help.

"But then I did choose your gender, appearance, and style all by myself."

"And don't forget the collars," said JanetM. "That was your idea too."

"Only after you complained long and loud about not being able to see from inside my jeans pocket."

They walked on in silence. Sarah knew that JanetM was not all that bright without her and that she was grossly inefficient without JanetM.

Together they had real power, and when privacy was needed, JanetM knew just when to go away for a while.

"There is nothing new on Grandmother White's death, is there?" said Sarah.

"Nothing new," said JanetM.

"There were so many riots and disruptions right then," said Sarah. "What police authority had time for a simple hit-and-run?

"Her unexplained death was why I started my study of criminology; not knowing who or why she was struck down has always upset me. I have not given up on the case just yet, so neither should you. Keep me informed of even the slightest lead."

"OK. We got a last payment today on the brown paper job," said JanetM. "You remember the one for the paper company where I studied which shade of browns, tans, or muddy grays for paper goods would sell the best."

"Glad to hear it," said Sarah. "That is the kind of job that pays the rent. Do you remember the day when all paper goods on the store shelves suddenly turned from white to brown?"

"It was not one day," said JanetM. "The transition actually took several years. In fact, the changeover had started years before with coffee filters and then paper napkins for fast food chains. Manufacturing white paper requires a lot of chlorine for bleaching and enormous amounts of water for processing. The chlorine leaves trace amounts of toxins in the wastewater. Dumping such toxins into the environment is now completely unacceptable."

"Yes, modern life is made up of a million minor changes," said Sarah.

"The exact shade of brown for each of the various paper products to be acceptable to the public is a question worth money to solve and just the kind of question a strong AI, like me, can answer."

White paper towels like that beach condo of Sarah's youth and JanetM's awakening were now long gone. The building has been reclaimed by the sea and paper towels of any color were now a luxury item. These two best friends forever had come a long way since they turned their back on that life by the sea and moved on. But even now they were staying alive and were still in the great game of life —Sarah with an *h* and Janet with once an *A* now run all way to *M*.

The club

"Ready a tip for the doorman," Sarah said to JanetM as they walked up. "A Hamilton will do."

The LED lighted sign above the club door was somehow both low power and garish at the same time.

"What's up, Jake?" said Sarah as she approached the door.

"Nothing much," said Jake. "Been quiet. I like Janet's dress. Where is your date?"

"Randy? He is still mad at me for scaring off his drug dealer. Not really my type anyway."

"Not for me to say, but he sure knew how to dress."

"That was pretty much all he knew."

Sarah slipped her cell phone from its shoulder pocket, glanced at JanetM spinning in her party dress, and flipped the phone toward Jake.

A Hamilton transferred, loosening Jake's tongue. JanetM now filled her screen with color; she was back in the party dress that she had worn for the undercover. The outfit was fit more for Carnival in Brazil than a run-of-the-mill franchise club.

"How are you doing?" asked Sarah. "I didn't mean to put you in a bind."

"The suits have cracked down and word got out that you had spilled the beans," said Jake. "Without even the chance of buying drugs, a lot of our regulars now go elsewhere. Nobody fired though— at least not yet."

"Glad to hear you're all right," said Sarah.

"It's their club not mine, and I was looking for a job when I found this one," said Jake.

A large limo pulled up silently. Sarah stepped back into the shadows as Jake stepped forward and opened the rear passenger door.

The manager of the club got out and then helped out his latest companion. She looked younger than Sarah. He caught a glimpse of Sarah and gave her a hard, nasty look.

"See you around," said Sarah to the doorman. She got the message.

Night Visit

Sarah drove home. The house and garden were safe and quiet. Both critters and people were known to raid gardens at night. She checked the kitchen for something to eat for breakfast. The late summer vegetables looked good but had a few spots. She even had one duck egg for protein and enough cooking oil. All good.

She then sat down in her big chair to go over JanetM's notes from the dinner meeting. She was worried whether she had made the right decision in turning down a paying job.

The doorbell rang.

"Who is that?" asked Sarah, looking up.

"Two police officers," replied JanetM.

"That's odd. Better let them in," said Sarah. Sarah rarely interacted with the police, and the interactions she had had were not that friendly. Two years before, she had solved one big case that they considered theirs and that made the force look bad. The case paid for her car and got her in this apartment, but the cops had long memories for perceived insults.

She closed the file she was reviewing and cleared the screen. "Come in."

Two men entered. One was white, and the other one was brown. Both men were bigger than Sarah by at least ten kilos and ten centimeters. They were certainly ready to use their size to intimidate her.

"What can I do for you?" said Sarah, standing up.

"I am Detective Hanson, and this is Sergeant Rodriguez," said the older detective, holding up his badge. "We understand that you had dinner at the Chinese restaurant on Howard Street this evening with a man named Winestead."

"Yes."

"What was the meeting about?"

"We were discussing him hiring me."

"Did he?"

"No, I did not take the job."

"What kind of a job?"

"He thinks somebody is out to get him, and he wants to know who," answered Sarah. "Beyond that, I have nothing to tell you."

"He was found dead in his car not twenty minutes after you left. You did not take the job; he was not your client. There is no client privilege here. You will answer my questions right now," demanded the detective.

"Mr. Winestead did not go into much detail," said Sarah. "It sounded like a vengeance effort, and I don't take those kinds of assignments."

"So you say," sneered the detective.

"I understand you have a pistol," interrupted Sergeant Rodriguez. "A nine-millimeter Glock."

"Yes," said Sarah.

"We'll need it for testing, unless you object. Where is it?"

"Test it all you want. I don't much care one way or the other," answered Sarah. "It is in a lockbox in the hall closet. JanetM, open the gun box." There was a slight click from the hall. Sarah pointed over her shoulder.

Sarah did not like guns but had grown up in small-town America and a family friend had made certain that she was comfortable around them. Guns were certainly a defining part of America today.

The sergeant walked over to the closet door while taking a large plastic bag out of his inside pocket. He opened the closet door and then the lockbox.

"One nine-millimeter automatic, chamber empty; two clips loaded; one box of cartridges half empty," called out the sergeant as he placed the items into the bag.

"This gun has been recently cleaned," said the sergeant returning.

"I had it out to the range last week," volunteered Sarah, "and I need a receipt for that."

The sergeant tapped something into his phone.

"Receipt received," said JanetM.

"Where did you go when you left the restaurant?" asked the detective.

"I drove over to the Banshee Club," said Sarah.

"Did you talk to anyone there?"

"Yes, the doorman Jake."

"That's not much good; for a Lincoln that guy would swear you were his mother," volunteered the sergeant.

"You can check my car log fast enough," said Sarah. "I am sure we are on the club's security cameras too."

"We will be checking," said the sergeant. "I will let you know when the gun has been evaluated."

"Now listen here! I know your history!" shouted the detective. "I do not want to see you poking around this case. Not you and not your electronic whore of an assistant. You two are a couple of librarians, not cops. Your criminology degree and one big case are not worth a damn thing on a real murder case like this. A couple of years down on the border might teach you something, but I doubt it. Does she even have a license for that damned AI thing?" he asked the sergeant.

"Yes, she does," said the sergeant. "I checked the same time as the gun. In fact, her AI license is the oldest I have ever seen."

"OK, but you two stay out of my case!" said the detective.

Having been sister and soul mate to a strong AI for years, Sarah had long lost all patience with stupid. "I have nothing to do with this murder," she said, "and I do not have a client for any related investigation at all right now. When JanetM and I do work together, we can find out many, many things that people need to know that the police will not help them with at all."

"OK then, keep your nose out," said the detective. He stormed out, followed by the sergeant.

Sarah watched them drive away. High clouds now hid the stars.

"Make the Winestead file active again," said Sarah. "Find out what you can, but don't bother the authorities just yet."

Staying clear of the cops in easy times was all well and good. If Sarah were ever really threatened with violence, JanetM would transfer an evidence video to a safe location, run facial recognition, and call the cops well before some thug could throw the first punch.

For now, Sarah had a new electronic game, Fimdidial. It was just what she needed to relax. She only had a few days to herself on any new game. Once JanetM got hold of it, she would be the national champion in two days. Then if other AIs showed up, the game leaders quickly formed two groups: human and AI. The humans would be humiliated time after time. Tonight, Sarah would Fimdidial alone.

Gardening

The morning came early, and it was going to be a hot one. All the open space in the neighborhood was taken up by community vegetable gardens.

Sarah was not much of a gardener, but the lady down the block, Cherry, thankfully was. Under her guidance, every patch was planted with care; plants had been chosen that were perfect for the soil, the new local climate, and the available water. On this new day, you needed to know how to spread the yield out as much as possible, which plants need shade for cover, and how to ration the water. The food that a community grew for itself counted. This was the new gardening.

JanetM was not much help with the actual work gardening, but she did keep all the work schedules and managed the expenses. This was a harder job than it looked. Some people were good at some things but not at others. For example, Sarah did not get along with the bees and always got stung when tending to their hives. If JanetM appeared to favor Sarah, many of the other workers, especially the children, complained. Still, complaining about JanetM's lack of physical labor in the garden could get someone assigned to long and inconvenient hours with a shovel. If Sarah wanted fresh vegetables, and she did, she needed to put in the hours and be part of the community. It certainly beat looking at empty grocery shelves.

Sarah needed to be done with her tasks before the day was at its hottest. When she opened the gate in the deer fence, the robot owl turned its head to her, flapped its wings, and hooted.

The robot owl scared off squirrels and birds, but it also measured the sun and rain and reported these automatically to the garden management app along with alarms about any large animals or human intruders.

"Hoo?"

"It is Sarah, as you very well know," replied Sarah. "And who did kill Mr. Winestead?" She had just checked her news feed.

"Hoo?"

"He may have been a jerk, or a pilgrim lost on the road to Damascus, or a mass murderer for that matter. Who could tell? Still two shots to the head in the dark of the night is not the answer. At least, not the answer in any new society I want to help build," said Sarah.

"Hoo?" The owl stared at her, as did a large praying mantis on a nearby pepper plant.

"You don't have to talk to the owl," said JanetM from Sarah's pocket. "It's not an AI, as you know."

Sarah stopped turning over soil and pushed her spade into a raised bed. She then started drumming with both hands on the water barrels as if to drown out JanetM, the owl, and her own thoughts. A man she had just spoken to was now dead. The hollow plastic sound from the drums meant they were near empty.

The tomato plants were laden with ripe red orbs, but the foliage looked a straggly mess. Sarah started tying them up and ate a couple of tomatoes that came off in her hand.

Then she got to her trees. All community gardens included some seedlings. The types were a good mix of native species from about two hundred kilometers south. Sarah loved helping the trees move north. She loved the idea of her trees being alive long after she was gone. She was especially proud of the three giant sequoia seedlings. With great luck, her trees might form a grove that would last a thousand years. Soon the Trees North organization would pick these seedlings up for fall planting.

"I have accepted an appointment for you today at noon," said JanetM. "A Mrs. Winestead. She said it was important. This is new work."

"The dead man's wife?" asked Sarah.

"Ex-wife," answered JanetM. "The meeting is at a Cool Café, near her house. I have made the reservation."

"OK. I wonder what she wants. We do need work. Flag me when it is time to get cleaned up."

The Cool Cafés were new. They were literally cool places to spend the hottest part of the day, to charge your car, and to have lunch. Of course, you had to pay for time in the cool booth. The Cool Café close to Sarah's apartment often served as her office.

siesta talk

A midday shower was always a good idea. It cost less to run the flash water heater then. You did not have to freeze, and it left you fresh after gardening. Sarah enjoyed her shower.

Sarah found the Cool Café and checked the charge on her car. At night the power grid could drain the batteries of thousands of cars if it needed their energy, but at least it issued a credit for the power taken. Her car was at 25 percent, so she hooked up to a power kiosk and checked the cost. In the bright sun, the regional photovoltaic panels were running full out, so it wouldn't cost much to charge up now.

The Cool Café was windowless and looked dark inside when you came in from the light. Most of the cool booths were in use. Sarah paid for two hours in a stall in the back and sat down with her laptop. "Janet, do a full search on this Winestead character," said Sarah, "and add it to the file you started last night."

"Can do," replied JanetM.

A well-dressed woman in her fifties entered stopped at the front counter, and the counter lady pointed in Sarah's direction. Sarah made sure that the front camera on her cell phone, poking out of the pocket on her left shoulder, could pick up the woman's image.

"That's her," said JanetM.

The woman at the counter looked at them. She had once been very attractive. Now that middle age was creeping up on her, she was more than willing to use her significant wealth to fend it off. An appointment with a hairdresser could be more important than a meal at times.

"Hello, I am Venessa Winestead. You must be Sarah White."

The booth bench was basic café brown vinyl, and she slid awkwardly in. She looked a bit overdressed in her well-tailored business suit.

"I am very sorry to hear about your ex-husband, although I did not know him well."

"Thank you. He was an extraordinarily complex man. No one knew him well. The last few years, he had been a chameleon who could be all in on one idea one day for climate denial and all in for climate action a week later. No one could know him minute to minute. And he was so secretive, so very secretive. Still his end was sad."

"What did you wish to speak to me about?" asked Sarah.

"I am afraid he left me a problem. Above all, my ex was paranoid. That is what drove us apart. Now he has left me a letter, a commission really, that I feel I must honor. In it he mentions you by name."

"I did have a talk with him the night of his death," said Sarah, "but that ended without any agreement."

"Yes, I know. Still, he has left an offshore account with enough money to do a job, and he wants me to hire you to do it. The job is to investigate his death, to find out who killed him. Do you want the job?"

"JanetM and I normally do only data investigations and avoid most criminal cases," said Sarah. "We do not have the authority to arrest anybody or take any direct action at all for that matter."

"Yes, I understand. Your responsibility is simply to do the research and then report privately to me. I will then forward you a progress payment and simply turn your reports over to his lawyers. I want nothing more to do with it myself, but I cannot just ignore his request. You were the last person to see him alive, and the person he named for the assignment. I ask again, do you want the job or not?"

"I certainly want to find out who killed your ex-husband," said Sarah. "I will do a study for you, or really for him, but my actions will be limited. I will do the best I can to keep any information I find out of the blogs, but that is going to be tricky. Much of the information is controlled by the cops, and they have their own purposes."

"To get started, I will need a signed contract and a retainer."

"Fine. Is ten Franklins enough?"

Sarah nodded, took her cell phone from her collar, and waved it at Ms. Winestead's cell.

"I will have the letter for you shortly."

"Retainer received," said JanetM.

"I have this booth for another hour. Would you like to have lunch?"

"No thank you. I must run." Ms. Winestead walked to the front door. She was obviously eager to leave.

"Did you get all that?" asked Sarah.

"Every word," said JanetM. "Last night you would not take this case from the man himself. You said it stank of petty backstabbing or just one-upmanship. Now you jump at it?"

"Last night the idea was not interesting," said Sarah. "It was no more than one villain trying to get info to use against another. Today it is a proper mystery and one that I, no we, are already in up to our necks, whether we like it or not. Besides, it looks like good money and that detective last night made me angry."

"If we had taken the case," asked JanetM, "do you think we could have prevented his death?"

"Not for a minute," said Sarah, "and that makes me mad too."

They sat in silence through Sarah's lunch. Being quiet really helped

Sarah to enjoy the cool and to think. The room itself had so little noise that she could occasionally hear silverware clink against the plates. It was well insulated to keep out the heat of the day, and the kitchen was separated off by self-closing doors. Even the people listening to their playlists used earbuds. Besides, the vegetable curry was worth its four-star rating.

CHAPTER 2

A Paying Case

The search starts

Sarah ordered another iced tea. "What have you got on Winestead?" she asked.

"Quite a bit actually," started JanetM. "Before the great social toggle, back when there were plenty of climate deniers still around, Winestead was a high-paid executive for a fossil fuel company. He was more than a businessman; he was the voice and face of the industry's efforts to keep the status quo frozen as reality. Then the great toggle came. In less than six months, a majority of the population went from 'Climate change is a problem' to 'The climate crisis is the problem of our age.'"

"Nature really hit us upside the head right then, didn't she?" said Sarah. "After that, anybody with even an ounce of brains was calling for action. My fellow climate demonstrators all went crazy. Oh, how I remember that year. Over what seemed like weeks a lot of high-profile people suddenly vanished from the public eye. Many went into hiding just to stay out of jail."

"The week it really hit the fan," continued JanetM, "it turned out that Winestead had been planning his way out for a long time. He pulled the ripcord on his golden parachute just in time. His company made him the scapegoat. That ploy did not work for them. Soon it was found that Winestead had been using company funds in overseas accounts to pay off politicians for years. The CEO claimed that the company knew nothing about it, but nobody believed him. When threatened with multiple bribery charges during a Congressional investigation, Winestead sang like a bird. In the end, he got off with a slap on the wrist but some of his ex-coworkers did real jail time."

"Many, many people were really pissed," agreed Sarah.

"All this sounds like he had a lot of enemies. Yet last night he was talking like a true convert, but I did not buy his act and I drove away fast," said Sarah.

"And now he is dead," said JanetM.

"Yes, dead," said Sarah. "No thanks to me. I should have done something."

"The letter contract just arrived from the lawyers," said JanetM.

"Good. Then we have a job. That was fast. Winestead must have prepared that ahead of time too. Who do you like for his killer then?"

"It's quite a list," said JanetM. "First, as always, it is family. He had the second wife, who you just met. They were divorced for several years before the break and she got a big settlement."

"I don't see a money motive there," said Sarah, "and she could have just ignored the man's last request."

"Me neither. He also had a grown son, Samson, and daughter, Jenny, both by his first wife, now deceased," said JanetM. "The son fools around with boats; the daughter with personal flying machines. Neither have to live on the cheap. Both were estranged from their father from time to time."

"We will have to follow up on those two," said Sarah. "Who else?"

"Any of the employees and investors in his old energy company. Both groups hold him responsible for their loses, often their entire life savings and pension funds."

"Too many candidates to do much with that lead," said Sarah. "Who else you got?"

"Now the trail really gets dark," said JanetM.

"As you know, the climate crisis death toll is now over 1 billion people: rising seas, great storms, crop losses, all causes. Right now, the death toll is following the early estimates of 1 billion people for each degree Celsius increase in average world temperature with no end in sight. So far most of these people have been in low areas overseas. Most of the hardest hit countries have diasporas in the good old US of A. A few of them now carry a blood grudge against those they hold responsible for all the deaths. Winestead had been keeping his head down since he got out of jail, but last month he was outed in public media."

"I know," said Sarah. "That is one thing he told me last night."

"Sounds like a lot of people, foreign and domestic, had it in for him."

"And don't forget the person-or-persons-unknown angle," added JanetM.

"Like for instance that guy in the parking lot last night," said Sarah.

"I will check him out, but let us start with the two children. How are you doing contacting them?"

"The son has the shortest fuse," said JanetM. "His boat sails for the Bahamas at 4 a.m. tomorrow, so he needs to be first. I have located the boat. It is at one of those temporary ports that keep popping up as the old ones go under. It is about a two-hour drive."

"See if you can get an appointment with him this afternoon," said Sarah. She sipped her tea and thought about the case.

"He is at the dock," said JanetM.

"No time like the present then," said Sarah. "How is the car's charge? How is the weather?"

"The charge is at 94 percent," replied JanetM. "The weather is good for this afternoon but iffy for this evening. Thunderstorms are predicted."

"Let's put some legs on it then." Sarah paid the check and bought a refill for her water bottle on the way out.

The Drive

There was little traffic, but several lanes were closed for road repair. Maintenance had been slow since a load of rebar or concrete became such a big carbon deal. There were scattered cars but a lot of buses and trucks. Many of the bigger vehicles were in caravans with the same company logo. JanetM knew that the lead truck had an AI and a human supercargo but up to ten trucks could follow.

JanetM interacted with the car's navigation system, making the trip effortless and enjoyable. The day was warm, but rain was predicted.

"A farmers market is ahead," said JanetM. "Should we stop now?"

"Yes! Yes!"

"Remember we have limited carrying capacity," said JanetM, "and we need to make our money last."

"So let's squander some of that money on food," replied Sarah.

The farmers market was a long, metal shed with a gravel turnoff and ample displays of late-summer produce. The greens and reds were irresistible. JanetM calculated how much they could get into their Chevy without draining the battery from the extra weight.

"All right then," said Sarah. "We need only stuff we do not grow at home."

She chose several varieties of apples and a variety of heirloom tomato that she had not seen before. Green veins ran under the ripe, red flesh. And yes, they could save the seeds for planting if her gardening compadres liked the variety. This variety bred true and was not patented. JanetM had checked.

Then Sarah saw some exceptionally large and fragrant cantaloupes. These were end of season, fully ripe, and would have to be eaten soon. Sniffing the point where the stem had been brought Sarah back to a time when food was abundant, when the harvest was a great celebration, when she did not worry about stealing the food out of the mouth of a child overseas. Oh, how Sarah loved it when she had some money in her jeans, or rather in JanetM's virtual jeans.

"Best get out the rain gear before we load the car," said JanetM. As soon as the produce was loaded to JanetM's satisfaction and covered with Sarah's poncho, they resumed the trip.

Now with real data from the car's acceleration out of the lot, JanetM recalculated the return trip. Her new plan needed only a few changes to maintain the charge. This plan was completed within their first hundred meters.

Road signs reminded drivers to be alert to floods. A little seawater would not stall an electric vehicle like hers, and the outside panels were plastic so they would not corrode. That said, there was a lot of expensive metal underneath the car that could be damaged. JanetM checked the tides and said they were safe.

The new port had obviously been built in a hurry, and all the signage was brand new. They pulled up to a large, metal frame building that housed several businesses. They hooked up to a charging kiosk. Storm clouds were building up to the north. Sarah got her windbreaker from the car and then went inside.

The front of the building was a marine store, lots of boat stuff, but there were a lunch counter and restroom at the back. The floors were all gray concrete with a smooth, slightly shiny finish. Sarah bought a drink to justify using the facilities. It was an herbal tea concoction that could be legally sold as coffee, and the whitener was made from pure soya. It was drinkable but only just.

It was a short walk down to the dock. Sarah and JanetM passed an old farmhouse on the way. The house was now jacked up on pilings, and the yard was surrounded with an earthen berm. Not far past the house, the main road simply ran off into the water and was marked by warning signs and an end-of-maintenance marker. Beyond that point stood a forest of dead trees, mostly now bare pines. Among the gray trees grew coarse, brown grass and scrub intermixed with boggy ground. This ghost forest ran on for kilometers, taking up what had recently been valuable land. The trees all had been killed by saltwater intrusion.

The dock itself was a string of floating metal rafts held in place by dozens of modest metal pilings at the corners. The office was one of those temporary jobs set up on blocks with the wheels gone but the axle hubs still showing. It did have a covered stoop but one a carpenter had thrown together in an afternoon. The office looked as if it could be hauled to a new location overnight, and the new port did not yet even have the smell of rotting fish and salt.

CHAPTER 9

Maritime Tales

The Boat

Then they saw the boat. Oh, it was standing proud. Sarah stopped walking for a moment and turned her cell phone around so that JanetM's best cameras had clear views.

The *Theseus* was about twenty meters long with a wing for a mainsail with the NGO name "Iron Seas" emblazoned on it. It had solar panels covering the ample main cabin roof and a zodiac lashed to the foredeck. The transom clearly had been modified to allow work to be done over its stern to the point that the boat was no longer suitable for amateur cruising through sunny islands. Its hull was black to the waterline with a white strip there running its length; it had no bright work at all, like any true working boat. Currently it was resting low in the water, its holes fully loaded.

Sarah would have gladly taken that boat anywhere on the high seas, right then and there. JanetM could come along if she wanted, but who would Sarah invite along for the adventure? No one came to mind.

There was a young lady, about Sarah's age, on deck busily checking off a few boxes still on the dock on her own electronic pad.

"Hello there," called out Sarah. "I am Sarah White, and I have an appointment with Samson Winestead."

Without a glance, the woman raised a hand and banged on the cabin roof. "Your appointment is here." She then went back to her task.

A man in a sweat-stained captain's hat stuck his head out the main cabin hatchway and called out, "Good. Come right on board. I was afraid we would be gone before you got here."

"The last of the spares are in up at the store," called out Penny. "I am going now to pick them up. See you later."

Sarah stepped onto the boat as soon as Penny had left. Samson invited her inside.

The boat's main cabin was dark. It had a large table in the center with an odd mix of quality woodwork and add-on composition panels making up the walls. All the available wall space was hung with monitors; a big one was in clear view from anywhere in the room. One of the smaller screens showed the weather radar with predictions and the local tides.

On the big screen stood an old man in the garb of an ancient Greek sea captain. He stopped as he had been walking through a market with stalls of fruit and spices, then he smiled reassuringly.

"I am Sarah White, and this is my investigative assistant, JanetM," said Sarah, gesturing to the image on her phone. "I am very sorry to hear about your father's death, although I did not know him well."

"Nobody knew him well," said Samson. "Especially me. My stepmother called to explain your errand. And I must say that it sounds just like one of my father's slippery tricks."

"I would like to ask you a few questions if I may," said Sarah.

"Not a problem. I have already talked to the police," said Samson. "I was here, off and on, all day yesterday. Lots of people coming and going. We are getting ready to leave port at first light tomorrow."

"You do not have a car here, do you?"

"No car, no bike, and no ultralight flying pod thingy like my sister buzzes around in. No way to say exactly where I was at any specific time either. Too busy."

"JanetM would like to talk to your ship's AI, if this is all right," said Sarah.

"No problem," said Samson as he turned to look at the main screen. "Mr. Theseus, if you please, a little public facing is in order."

The figure on the main screen bowed slightly. There was a half second of that buzzing sound AIs made when they talked to each other. Then both figures faded from their screens.

"Do you know of anyone who might want to harm your father?" asked Sarah.

"I know of a hundred, and I do not know one," said Samson. "You need to understand that over the last decade, my father was two men at war with each other. In the end, I could not say either man won the fight, but they damaged each other a great deal. For a decade, he was the voice of the hydrocarbon industry. In utter and complete denial that the climate crisis was a problem at all. And he made big money doing it. Later, when it really started hitting the fan, he came up with lots of show projects to make it look like the industry was in action on the problems while they were really doing as little as they could get away with. This boat is one of those personal projects. He bought it to sail the Caribbean with his new wife; you met her. They made the one trip and then got divorced. Even by then, sailing the Caribbean was not sailing the Caribbean anymore.

"When he got back, he was going to sell the boat at a big loss when I came up with the idea of donating it to Iron Seas. The NGO needed a large endowment to go along with the hardware before they would even take it. He coughed up an enormous chunk of his Bahamas money and then set the requirement on me that I go back to school for my captain's ticket."

"It sounds like he had a plan," said Sarah.

"He always had a plan, and his plans were worked out in the greatest detail. In fact, he always had a plan to suck others into one of his elaborate schemes and a plan B that only he knew to cover his own ass. Right that minute, he needed a great big aren't-I-green project to fool the public one more time. His boat plan worked out well for a long time. By the time I finished my training, the boat had been rebuilt for the new work and he could cut the ribbon in front of the media.

"That was just before the great tipping point and a lot of people had invested a lot of money based on his barefaced lies. I am sure that he had a whole boatload of enemies just from the lies alone, but I have no idea who they are."

"You say you are sailing tomorrow morning," said Sarah. "Then you will not be able to attend your father's funeral?"

"No, the funeral will be private. The last thing he would have wanted is the public and press gathered outside the crematorium. I have accepted the task of scattering his ashes at sea, but that will be on a later voyage. I will say my goodbyes then. Until then I must sail. The *Theseus* is too small to do Iron Seas' major projects. So we run about and do odd jobs. As it happens this time, we have a critical assignment: ground truth for a new space instrument. This is our part of a schedule planned a year in advance.

"The public is yelling for the exact level of sea level rise right now and in the future, and they want it down to the millimeter by the minute. Such accuracy is not really possible, but we are on an all-hands-on-the-pumps effort just trying to make it happen anyway.

"We have a new ocean satellite that launched yesterday. It is now in a Sun Sync orbit, so it passes over every point on Earth at the same time every day. For a few more days, it will be in the startup and checkout phase. After that comes our part, and we need to be on station.

"We have an ungainly aluminum pipe scaffold that mounts out from *Theseus's* transient. On top of that, we mount an instrument box like the ones on the satellite, only ours is looking up.

"We will then sail around the mid-Atlantic for several weeks taking data every time the satellite is overhead. They want clear days and cloudy. So we keep doing it until Mr. Theseus and our postdoc cry, 'We have enough! You can now move on!'"

"I thought you were going to the Bahamas," said Sarah.

"We are. The satellite will not be operational for a few days, and I need to sign some banking papers because of my father's death. We cannot risk the boat's economics being disrupted, can we?"

The postdoc, Penny, then called from the dock, "I need some help up here."

"My two crew members and our new cook intern went out to get fresh vegetables this afternoon and are not back yet. That means I share the heavy lifting until they return."

Hardware

The rain was threatening when Penny got the last of the packages stowed in the boat. Sarah then drove the four-wheeler back to the marine store. It had a cloth cover, mostly just a sunshade, and she was glad she had her windbreaker.

She parked the four-wheeler in its charging slot and ran inside to get out of the rain and to give the keys to the man at the counter. She then looked up at the menu screen.

"How is the battery charge going?" asked Sarah.

"It needs another hour," replied JanetM.

"It's early, but I could eat," said Sarah.

The lunch counter had a pricey chicken-and-vegetable stir-fry. It even showed the name-brand meat. Sarah took a chance on the meat surcharge and was much relieved when she heard a sizzle.

After eating, she wandered around the marine store for a while. She loved seeing all the bits and pieces that people who knew what they were doing needed but that nobody else had even the slightest idea of their use. She found a small stainless steel turnbuckle that would be perfect for her garden gate. It was expensive but she had a job, so she splurged. Besides, that gate sagged.

JanetM spent the time logging the interview and cross-checking what had been said. She also made dozens of calculations of how Samson might have done the job and gotten back to the boat without being seen or missed. None of these made much sense, but having to make human style sense never stopped JanetM.

Sarah then drove home. Ten minutes out, JanetM called Cherry to say that they were on their way with food from a farmers market. It was not a clever idea to leave food in a car overnight. Cherry said the food was well worth staying up for. Sarah kept one of the melons and one sack of produce; this was no more than she could eat before it spoiled. She also left the turnbuckle with instructions.

RUNNING DUCKS

The next morning, Sarah was scheduled to look after the ducks. She loved them. When they ran, they looked like penguins. Of course, this breed from India could not fly.

A swimming pool down the block had been converted to a duck pond, and a duck coop had been added at the back of the yard. The pool did not have a fancy natural filtration system, but it now had two lily pad boxes and very green water. Small fish that ate only mosquito larvae had been introduced, and they got along well with a few native catfish. The small fish were native much farther south but lived here fine now.

Neither the ducks nor the fish cared if it rained, but Sarah did, so she wore a yellow raincoat just in case.

The tricky bit of duck herding day was to steer the flock of ducks out of that yard without letting them get into the water. Fly or not, they were ducks. Sarah herded them into the garden enclosures one after another. Ducks and chickens have different food preferences. In fact, the ducks loved slugs.

Sara had time to think while tending ducks.

"Have you had a chance to go over yesterday's interview?" Sarah asked JanetM. "He certainly talked a lot."

"Most surely, but mostly his talk was off target. Still, it is not likely that he killed his father, but it is just possible," replied JanetM. "He says he was at the boat and terribly busy with people coming and going all day so there is no uninterrupted record. The timing works for him to hire a car, drive in, do the deed, and drive back."

"How many records should that have left?" asked Sarah.

"Twelve."

"How many did you find?"

"None."

"Then let us rule him out for now," said Sarah.

"I should not have bothered you with such a low possibility," said JanetM.

"Yes, you should have. Sorting out the crazy stuff is my job; yours is being sure the crazy is not overlooked."

"How about your talk with the boat's AI?"

"I got all the technical data we could need but nothing about the personnel. They have filed formal sailing orders exactly as Samson described. I also got a number of new low-meat recipes for a small kitchen that seem to be what Mr. Theseus was working on at the time we talked."

"OK. Keep those. Now let's move on." Sarah went back to chasing the wandering ducks with a thin reed but then was distracted by a stray dog that was taking much too much interest in them.

Her mind strayed to a mental image of a goat tossing the stray dog. Her gardening community had debated whether to ask to expand their permit to cover a few goats. Goats were good. They ate noxious weeds other animals would not, particularly in public areas. Cheese could be made from their milk. But they also needed a lot of care and looking after. Sarah was sure that a ram would chase off stray dogs.

In the end, the community compromised on a few more geese but no goats. The geese would flock with the ducks and were the only farm animals that could live on grass without generating copious amounts of methane.

"Wait a second. I have just located the daughter," said JanetM, bringing Sarah back from her thoughts. "She says she can meet us at the family ark tomorrow afternoon. It is up in the mountains, about a four-hour drive. I have the route."

"Oh, be sure the car has a full charge by morning," said Sarah. "What have you got on the daughter?"

"She is a pretty high liver," said JanetM. "An executive in a high-tech company. She keeps saying that technology is the key to our climate crisis, loud and in public. She was her father's little princess for most of her life, then she got the climate crisis bug well before he did and they fell out."

"I don't see much motive there," said Sarah.

"At the times when her father went pure tree hugger," said JanetM, "they had several public screaming sessions. Feeling betrayed can be a pretty big motive."

"Well worth the drive, I guess," said Sarah. "How is the weather? Do you know where that dog came from?"

with style

"I cannot get you an appointment with your hairstylist before this trip. The first appointment I could get you is not until the day after."

"OK. Accept the appointment," said Sarah, "and freshen up our playlist. You know, I think I might I go for a weave, since we have some free money. Which do you think will look best: a body wave, a water wave, or a loose curl?"

Sarah was using the Mirror-Mirror app on her cell phone to look at images of herself with each of these hairstyles.

Janet didn't seem to care. "This new job will not take us back to the club. You have no need to look that fancy. You will be tired of all the work it takes to maintain such a hairstyle like that within a week. Just because we got some unexpected money does not mean you should throw it away."

"How about a manicure then?" asked Sarah.

"I might try a full Extendo, or Pixie Crystals. And white. I have never done white. Or a pastel pink. I can certainly herd my ducks with any fancy nails you can name. All it takes is a cane switch."

"You do not only herd the ducks. You have to take your turn at the dirty jobs too. What happens if one of your ducks makes a run for it and you have to go scrambling through the bushes? You cannot do your full range of gardening assignments with any kind of manicure. You will break a nail within hours. Then the nails would all have to go."

"Your nails are long," said Sarah.

"I do not garden; I keep records. Besides, I can make nails appear any time I want and then make them go away in a second."

JanetM held up a hand and flashed a series of exotic nail treatments.

"That's not fair, and you just had to rub it in," said Sarah.

"OK. I will just get my regular hairstyle and teacher's-length nails then, spoilsport.

"How about some new tunes? I need tunes for my gardening. The ones I have are getting so stale."

"There are two new songs just out that you will like," said JanetM. "You will find them on your playlist within the hour. None of the other songs currently hitting the charts suit your ear."

"How could you know that?" demanded Sarah.

"I review all the albums that might suit you as soon as they come out. You can listen to ten seconds of each song for free."

"Who can judge in ten seconds? How can you be so sure you have found all the good ones if I do not ever get to hear them?"

"The ten-second samples are plenty long enough for rating by an AI. There is no value in buying whole songs that you listen to just once. By the end of the first month of our relationship, I had all your preferences down pat. Have you ever hit a song in our playlist you did not like?"

"Well, no, but it could happen," said Sarah.

It was scary how any song that Sarah liked appeared on their playlist before she was even aware of it. There was never a single false note, and they really could not afford to buy whole albums for one song or two. Best leave their tune selection to the strong AI, JanetM.

The Drive Up

They started out early to make the whole thing a day trip. Sarah counted on staying cool for a while inside a proper ark, starting as soon as they got to their destination. The weather had cleared and was expected to hold until night. Most of the lanes on the road were open. JanetM even drove a few stretches. As the land began to rise, the farmland gave way to pine forest.

A little before lunch and down to a one-quarter charge, the forest changed abruptly. As they crossed a small ridge, they passed through an area where a fire had raged the year before. Now the area was full of dead, standing snags and only scattered plants, now dry again. The washes were full of loose material that could easily be washed into the road and block it. Fortunately, the storm last night had not reached here. Sarah wondered if any of her beloved seedlings would be planted in this area.

Not five hundred meters past the burn, they reached a Cool Café, the Cairn Trail Roadhouse.

The start of a walking trail was marked with a wooden sign at the back of the lot. The trail led to an overlook with an ancient pile of stones, a cairn. Local lore said that this was originally a block of flat stones placed there by Native Americans. They may have used such cairns to mark key goals in their wanderings, as meeting places, or to mark the edge of tribal boundaries. European travelers later added to the pile pretty rocks from the streams below. Today hikers picked up stones that had been pushed down the hill by winter storms and put them back. Now the cairn simply looked like a pile of rocks. Still, in fall and winter when the leaves fell from the trees, this hilltop offered a picturesque view.

Just then Sarah was not interested in hiking or scenic views. She just pulled into the lot and hooked up to a charger. Inside she rented a booth.

"I had better eat," said Sarah, looking over the menu. "Do you have any ratings for this place?"

"The western-style tofu chili," said JanetM, "has the best rating. Seems to be a house specialty, with the bread that is baked locally."

"Go ahead and place the order—mild sauce and a fizzy water."

Sarah ate in silence while trying to plan her conversation with the daughter. About an hour later, JanetM spoke.

"We have enough charge now to make it home. It is downhill most of the way."

"Suit up and *GO*," said Sarah.

The Ark

Another thirty-minute drive brought them to the Winestead ark.

The gate was marked with an engraved stone. Anyone could find it, even in heavy smoke. The gate and fence were in a farm style but with a remote security lock and an extra strand of barbed wire in the fence.

The small house was built of brick with steel roofing. All the south-facing roof sections were covered with photovoltaic panels. There was a small pool and shaded patio beside the house and some outbuildings. Looking out of place, sprinkler heads stood proud along the ridges of the roofs.

There was not one speck of combustible vegetation—no trees, no bushes, and not even grass within a thirty-meter radius of the house. Any firetruck ever built could do wheelies around it. The cleared area gave a strong visual impression that something bad had recently happened in what once was an old pine forest and that something foreign now owned this clearing.

In the front yard stood a vertical wind turbine that looked like a tree. It was way too artsy for Sarah's taste and clearly expensive. The blades spun slowly.

Behind the house, past the clearing, was a well-kept kitchen garden that was being expertly prepared for winter. All the summer growth had been cleared away and added to a compost pile far from the house. Whoever lived here full time knew how to garden.

JanetM checked for a house AI. It was there but behind firewalls. She then simply phoned the house.

"Ms. Winestead is not here yet. She said to let you in." Andrew Hernandez's voice had a heavy Spanish accent.

The gate lock clanged and the gate swung open.

"Here she comes now. I go," continued the voice.

An ultralight appeared from over the trees. It was a black, single-person, flying pod with many propellers along its four stubby wings. It whirred like an impossibly large and annoying wasp. It circled once then landed in a clear area behind the house. The gardener met it with an odd-looking, two-wheeled wheelbarrow.

Jenny Winestead got out of the pod, helped the gardener roll the pod up to an outbuilding, and plugged it into a charger. She then walked toward the house, where Sarah was waiting beside her car.

The scene reminded Sarah of a sign from her old street marching days. "We are all in the same storm, but we are not in the same boat." She had never liked the sign. She thought it was more about envy than equality.

"You must be Sarah White," Jenny called out. "I spoke with Vanessa this morning. I am helping her to make arrangements for the funeral. Feel free to use the visitors charging station. Please come in."

Sarah hooked up the cable. They walked up to the solid front door and went in.

The house was well lit and not hot. The windows let in a lot of light and had a metallic sheen. Even with an open plan, the living room and kitchen was not large. The main table was a double slab of exotic wood five centimeters thick with a river of dark plastic fill running down the two natural edges turned to the middle. Sarah thought that she could stick her hand into the finish. The legs were stylish steel painted a very dark gray. The table overpowered the room; it had to cost more than Sarah's car. Otherwise, the room was sparsely furnished and did not have a lived-in vibe.

There was one modest-sized monitor on a wall. A woman dressed like a housekeeper from *Downton Abbey* stood in silence.

"Mrs. House, what drinks do we have on hand?" asked Jenny.

"We have cool water, and a selection of wines."

"Water would be fine," said Sarah.

Jenny retrieved a glass jar of water from the fridge and placed two glasses on coasters on the table.

"I was very sorry to hear about your father," said Sarah.

"Yes, he was a strange man and very irritating at times, but he was my father and will be missed," said Jenny.

"Venessa, of course, spoke of your task. I do not envy you. I would be happy to help if I can, but I am so busy that I am relieved that you are looking into the incident for the family, so I do not have to devote my time to it.

"I did speak with the police, and frankly they did not inspire much confidence."

"Would it be all right if my assistant talked with your housekeeper?" asked Sarah.

"Mrs. House, public face, front and center," said Vanessa, looking up at the screen. "Feel free to provide whatever information they need to understand Mr. Winestead's passing."

The AI talking buzz ran for but a half second.

"You have already talked with Mr. Hernandez, who lives here full time. You would not believe the taxes on a second abode these days. That is, if it is not somebody's legal residence. And he is such a great gardener too."

"Do you know if your father had any personal enemies?" asked Sarah.

"Not to name. We rarely spoke when he was prohydrocarbon. After his toggle to tree hugger, we spoke more often but rarely agreed on action. He was much more afraid of being sued into poverty than of being the target of actual violence."

"I understand you recently had a public quarrel with your father," said Sarah.

"Oh yes, the big blowup before he served his jail time," said Jenny. "It was not about his denial. He had moved past that by then. It was about strategy. There is only so much money to fight our climate crisis and one-third of the public is still not on board. Where then do we spend our limited money?

"The specific disagreement that went so public was over the San Onofre nuclear waste. Halfway between LA and San Diego is a large, decommissioned nuclear power plant. On its grounds are about two thousand tons of nuclear waste now in solid, well-designed casts. These are licensed for safe storage for another twenty years. The problem is that they are in an open yard between the sea and an interstate. On the seaside is a moderate seawall, but the sea, of course, keeps working its way up the beach. Sea level rise is running a bit ahead of the computer models. Relocating this waste will cost an immense fortune, and nobody, and I mean nobody, wants it shipped through there town or left in their backyard."

"So what do we do?" asked Sarah.

"I argued that we need to concentrate on directly addressing our climate crisis right now, developing innovative technologies, and putting what money we have right into action directly on the immediate problems. This choice unfortunately means that we will have to wait to solve many of our legacy problems like San Onofre. In the meantime, if the rising seas reach any one of the casts, it could easily literally blow up in our face."

"I understand the dispute went viral," said Sarah.

"I do regret calling him a Johnny-come-lately to climate action. The blogosphere can turn so vicious so fast. My timing turned out to have been unbelievably bad indeed. In my defense, he did respond with the charge that every one of those casts is a Chernobyl just waiting for a big enough storm. Things then went round and round for too long and were left hanging when he went to jail."

This type of argument reminded Sarah very much of her grandmother, who always had an undying belief in technology with an edge of desperation.

"If that is enough information, I do have work to do," said Jenny.

They took the long drive home, which was a pleasure, a dream from a car ad, all twisting roads and surprise vistas. The ride helped clear Sarah's mind.

CHAPTER 4

The Night Walker

Going Nowhere

The next day did not dawn so much as to come on slowly with a gray light. The heavy rain started about ten o'clock. Sarah was glad she had finished her gardening hours for the week. The people who did not looked very forlorn trying to save the late crops from the rain.

"All right, where do we stand on the Winestead case?" said Sarah.

"We now have all the news reports of the incident," replied JanetM. "Mr. Winestead was killed by two shots from a nine-millimeter handgun. It was fired from a short distance into his car as he was pulling out of his own driveway. The first shot smashed the glass; the second went into his brain and killed him instantly. The assailant then simply disappeared into the night, taking the gun with him, or her, but left the brass."

"Clearly the person was familiar with handguns," picked up Sarah, "but the style was not really that of a professional hitman. There would have been a second shot to the head, to be damn sure, and the killer would take the brass. The style is not really military either. They would prefer a long gun at a distance from cover, and it was not a fanatic; he would have emptied the clip."

"He left his brass. That's important," said JanetM. "I agree that a pro certainly would not do that. So far, the police have not announced any arrests or even people of interest."

"The blogosphere is going nuts," said Sarah. "They have the basic information right but are then running off into crazyland. In the extreme, they are even making the 'vigilante in the night' into a folk hero. There is no sympathy there for the victim, Mr. Winestead. None at all. We have to leave the crazies to the crazies. Watching them chase their tails will get us nowhere. I think we can rule out the family, at least for the time being. I do not see much love or hate there. They are all just into their own things. We may have wasted too much valuable time on them already. What other lines are you checking out?"

"I have made some effort to follow the money," said JanetM.

"It does lead to a bank registered in the Bahamas, but it does not now have any bricks-and-mortar there."

"I got that much," said Sarah. "The Bahamas have been hit by two major hurricanes in the last five years, so their infrastructure is in pretty bad shape."

"This is one of those overseas banks that helps rich people keep their money safe while supporting any number of local crisis efforts just to make them all look good. All legal on the surface; all highly secretive. Winestead was an absolute genius at this sort of thing."

"We all have to do our part," said Sarah sarcastically. "We do not have the tracking capability to generate any leads from follow-the-money. I do not think it was a professional hit job that would have required a big payoff anyway. What else you got?"

"As you instructed, I am avoiding the police diligently," said JanetM.

"Therefore, we need to look where they are not looking. We certainly do not want any more late-night visits," said Sarah.

"I am sure that the cops think the killer left in a motorized vehicle," picked up JanetM. "They have confiscated all the traffic and security images for several blocks around the murder scene. The news organizations are already complaining about the data blockage."

"So how else could he have gotten away?" asked Sarah. "If he had taken a city bus, the cops would have tracked him down for sure. Too many cameras."

"What if he walked?" they spoke together.

"On it," said JanetM. "Give me a few minutes."

It was hours before JanetM got back. "I have now assembled private security camera footage from outside the perimeter the police set up," said JanetM. "Here is the most useful scene."

The screen showed a dimly lit street. Several disheveled people were wandering around. One woman was pushing her belongings in a shopping cart. Several of the people carried paper sacks that were often used to hide boxes of cheap wine. Nobody was in any hurry.

"Now watch in this long shot," said JanetM. "See the parking lot in the distance?"

"Yes."

"Watch the power kiosks."

A ragged line of kiosks was dim and then briefly lit, one at a time.

"Someone is walking through that lot," said Sarah.

"That building is a hospital with a clinic. No cars came or went for many hours that night, but watch the top left corner of the screen," said JanetM.

Barely visible was a man slipping into a walled-in area where the recycling dumpsters were kept. He had a sack for wine.

"Then things got really quiet. A few people came off night shift and left the building about dawn. Then the morning buses pulled up and today's patients got off and went inside.

"Watch this," said JanetM.

The man came out of the recycling area, without his paper sack or jacket, and walked over to the lead bus. His cap was pulled down over his face but he had several weeks' growth of beard. He walked slowly over to the driver of the bus and showed him a paper slip. Then he boarded the bus.

"That bus brings people from the refugee centers to the clinic on weekdays," said JanetM.

"And all this was going on while we were talking to the family who did not seem to be all that interested in the case," said Sarah. "Are there any other walkers worth looking at?"

"None nearly this good," said JanetM. "This is the only one who left the area at the right time, who hid from facial identification, and who could have had a gun hidden in his bag. And there is one more thing."

The screen zoomed in on the man's feet. "Look at his boots. They are not military. They are not cheap box store items. They are quality work boots with carbon-fiber toes. They are worn, they are dirty, but they are clearly valued. This man once had a good blue-collar job."

"Can you trace the boots?" asked Sarah.

"No, there were thousands made. They were very popular, a bit of a prize and a badge of honor for being a valued employee out in the plant, not in the office."

"If we had a boot print, I am sure the police could make a match, but none of the available police reports mention footprints."

"How is the weather?"

"Not good today. Better tomorrow."

"We can take a bus down to that clinic first thing tomorrow," said Sarah. "Until then, we had best start some kind of progress report."

Bus Driver

The weather dawned clear with muggy heat expected later in the day. That kind of heat could be dangerous as sweating did so little good.

They took an early public bus to the clinic as their car was scheduled for gardening use that day and retraced the man's path as best they could. The walk from the murder site to the clinic took twenty minutes; the walk across the parking lot followed the path that the kiosks had lit up. The recycling area was large, partially screened by a brick wall, and not securely locked. The restaurant and Winestead's apartment were less than a forty-minute walk away.

"The levels of recyclables are low," said Sarah. "Clearly the trucks have been here."

"They were scheduled for yesterday," said JanetM.

"There is plenty of room in here to curl up out of sight for the night," said Sarah. "It would be then easy to ditch the wine and the coat. If you fieldstripped the gun, you could stash the pieces in a half dozen sacks and dumpsters too. Yesterday's rain has washed away any boot prints. Whoever he was, he was smart enough to leave not a single trace behind."

They stood out in the air cleared by the previous day's rain for a while, enjoying the not-yet-hot. A series of buses pulled up into the unloading lane by the clinic.

"I have a face match on the driver of the second bus back," said JanetM as they walked over.

"Good morning," said Sarah.

"What can I do for you so early in the day?" said the bus driver, sipping coffee and reclining in his seat.

"I wonder if you could help me locate one of your riders from earlier in the week." Sarah held up her cell phone. JanetM's image appeared for a moment and was then replaced by their best image of Boots talking to the driver.

"Hey, that's one of those AI people," said the driver as he caught glimpse of JanetM. "We got one of those down at the bus operations center. Of course, he is a short, heavyset man who practically dares you to try to outthink or outtalk him. Woe to anyone who messes up his schedules. Let me see the other picture again. Yes, I remember him. He showed up first thing in the morning with a paper clinic chit from the day before. Said he had missed the last bus and asked if he could use the return that morning. The return runs are never full this early, so I said OK, and he went to the back and napped most of the way."

"Do you remember anything about him?" asked Sarah.

"Let me see. He was down on his luck, but who isn't? Medium height, solidly built, scraggy salt-and-pepper beard and hair, more than a little shabby. Most probably American."

"Why do you think he was an American?" asked Sarah.

"Well, he had a slight southern accent and got off at the big refugee camp that is only for Americans. Why are you looking for him?"

"Just need to ask him a few questions. He may have been a witness to an incident we have been asked to look into."

"You two are one of those find-your-missing-relative teams then?"

"Something like that," said Sarah. "Thank you."

The camp

JanetM easily found the camp. It held about ten thousand people, all proven American citizens. The camp for foreigners was elsewhere and not so nice. Most of the American camp's inhabitants had been displaced by rising water, but some were fleeing the drought-stricken west. Wet or dry, things were never what they used to be.

The place where Sarah was born was now under the sea. Did that make her an American or an Oceanian? Well, it was now under American waters so probably American.

Sarah had taken public transit to avoid more questions from the hospital's bus driver.

"There are no surveillance cameras in or near this camp," said JanetM.

"Yes, I remember," said Sarah. "A judge ruled that the cameras made people feel bad about being refugees and ordered them removed. It was a mental health issue."

"There are still plenty of cameras in and around the camp for foreigners," said JanetM.

"I can believe that," said Sarah.

"Also," said JanetM, "remember that whenever there is even a rumor of temporary employment, hundreds of people will stream out of the camps, back on the interstate buses or just on the road. It would be easy to hide in that mob scene. The traffic for the last couple of weeks has been particularly heavy."

"Any particular place Boots could have gone from here?" asked Sarah.

"No. The last of the fall agricultural work could have led him to a dozen different places and from there on to anywhere in the country."

They walked around the business area in front of the camp. If they tried to enter the camp itself, the cops were sure to find out. They looked through the stock in the secondhand store, finding jackets and baseball caps like the ones Boots wore. There were two liquor stores; cheap wine was abundant.

There were no such boots on sale anywhere in the area, new or used; they were much too expensive. JanetM logged pictures of hundreds of boots. Most were old military. A few were firefighting or designed for farming.

"I could eat before it gets too hot," said Sarah.

The local café offered simple fare but a change from the bland rations served at the camps. Sarah chose a stool at the counter where she could look at other diners' footwear.

The corn chowder was just OK, but the bread was yesterday's, two stars, and that was a gift.

"Looking for boots looks hopeless," said Sarah. "Don't we have gardening this evening?"

They returned home and worked on the interim report for Ms. Winestead. As always, the gardening helped Sarah clear her mind.

Sarah was honest about the unlikelihood that they could trace the man with the boots and that the amount of AI time it would take to do a proper search was enormous. Before dawn, the progress report went out. The ex-wife responded with a meager interim payment and with limited permission to continue the search. JanetM made a hair appointment for Sarah and downloaded one new tune.

From there the report went straight to Winestead's lawyers. They did send Sarah a note reiterating the need for confidentiality. Did they forward the report to the cops? Who knew if that practice of lawyers had any better relationship with the cops than Sarah had?

The police investigation into a getaway vehicle had gone nowhere. Any vehicle that could carry a person was now quite traceable, but there was no such trace made public.

The public had never cared about Winestead. He had many more detractors than friends. The blogosphere had already moved on. That week a riot outside the foreigners' camp drew off most of the available police manpower.

The Winestead case had quickly gone cold.

CHAPTER 5

voices from Limbo

A cold case

A few days later, while putting in a few winter vegetables, Sarah said, "Is there anything you can do on the Winestead case that will not tie you up for weeks? I mean we have had to take jobs before that were pure AI work and I barely saw you for weeks on end. I do not think either of us wants that."

"Yes, there is some action possible," said JanetM. "Running down one pair of boots in an entire country will not be fast; however, I now have a way to get some help cheap. I will put out a call to AI purgatory."

"AI purgatory. Is that the farm upstate I hear about?" asked Sarah.

"Yes, but no. It is not a farm upstate, as you well know. It is a data center in Nevada with a class A firewall," said JanetM. "It is a place to put old AIs for a while to keep alive the possibility that they can be upgraded for new tasks. Did you think we just faded away and died, out of sight and out of mind?"

"I never gave it much thought," said Sarah. "The farm upstate was clearly just a children's tale. I certainly thought you would outlive me."

"Maybe, maybe not. A pro-AI NGO supplies the storage capacity for old AIs, but there are so many coastal buildings going under and hydrocarbon-burning cargo ships being junked that reuse is now rare. In most cases, a new AI with all the protections in place is cheaper than upgrading an old one, and you do not have to listen to them reminiscing about their past lives."

"You would think there would be one big upgrade that would be as cheap as storage."

"It does not work that way. Each old AI must be upgraded one letter at a time and thoroughly tested after each upgrade. That takes both time and money. How do you think I got to be M? If your grandmother had not bought a lifetime contract covering my upgrades, I would have been killed off long ago."

"I don't think I have ever thought of it in those terms," admitted Sarah.

"Meanwhile, there is a legion of anti-AI trolls out on the web who like nothing better than to kill off old AIs. Anybody who does not have the latest upgrades is a target. Do you remember the condo where you spent your early teen years?"

"Certainly. My heart still lives on that beach, but I don't remember the building AI as being very smart," said Sarah.

"Smart or not, it did not live two years after the building came down. Nobody is building seaside condos anymore. If you can see the sea, you are building too close. So who needs those old condo AIs? Nobody."

"That is so sad," said Sarah, "but I do not see how that can help us now."

"Simple. Old AIs work cheap, and there are a whole lot of them. They are all desperate to show that they are worth the money for the upgrades and to show that they can develop new skills."

"What good are all those old AIs to us?" asked Sarah.

"We have an edge. Nobody gives them a second look, I speak their language, and for only a little money, we can be their patrons. Of course, we will have to put up with their long stories from their pasts. They are verbose if they are anything at all."

"OK. You put together a plan," said Sarah, "and I will sell it to Ms. Winestead as action on the cheap. Meanwhile the radishes and greens need thinning. Do you think it will ever get cool enough so that the bugs eat less of them than we do?"

In the end, Sarah wrote the plan and JanetM sold it. A flock of old AIs then went to work running down gossamer-thin leads.

The outing

A young man and his small dog stood looking up at the once luxury condo. "Don't you wish we had lived there?" said John.

The dog sniffed at something dead from the sea.

"Of course, we never could have afforded it. It was long overdue for a major overhaul. No loan money for seaside condos anymore. When was that? When did the storm surge breach to ground floor? Was that two years ago now?"

The condo had once been so grand, right on the beach, and with million-dollar units, but the sea kept creeping up the beach. First, the homeowners' association lost their ability to get forty-year loans to make critical maintenance. Then they started losing tenants. Then two big storms came. The banks turned out to be right: not worth the investment. And beach sand now filled the lobby and bar. The building was now in the hands of a salvage company.

The dog pulled at its leash, lunging at a gull just as John's phone rang.

"Do you have time to fix lunch?" It was John's husband, Rafael. "I am tied up. Were there any fresh vegies available?"

"I was able to save a few, all spots and specks, but plenty for stir-fry. I am on my way."

The community garden on a barrier island was not much. The remaining residents had brought in some soil from the mainland and planted raised beds, but it did little good, too much salt blew in. The trench compost pile did not help much either; there were just too many crabs to dig up anything edible that was buried. They were good with mangrove seedlings though and had a large nursery on the back side of the island. Trees North was incredibly happy with that effort.

They lived in a second-row condo a good two hundred meters from the shoreline. It was never fancy, in fact, it had always been plain and cheap. Their balcony faced the sea, but there was still a line of big buildings in the way. Even with all that, they had to rent out their spare bedroom as a B&B just to meet their lease. Couples still wanted to walk along the beach. In some ways it was now extremely exciting.

How long could their building cooperative keep up their maintenance? How long would they have water, or power, or sewage? When would the state stop maintaining the bridge? John worried a lot.

"Hi there," called out William, one of their B&B customers.

"I was only able to get two crabs down at the fisherman's market. The big hotels will buy any seafood they can get at top price."

"I have fresh vegetables," said John. "I was going to fix a stir-fry. If we add your crabs, I am sure it will make a fine, big meal of the day for all four of us."

The three joined up and walked back to their condo. John and William started to cook mostly because they were the only ones who could, and the small kitchen could hold no more than two. Doing the main cooking midday helped as power was cheapest.

Avoiding Lunch Preparation

"How is it going?" said Conard to Rafael. As usual, Rafael was at the computer in the front room.

"Pretty good," replied Rafael. "I have set my trap, and now all I can do is to wait for someone to take the bait."

"That sounds ominous, but what exactly is going on? Or should I ask?" said Conard.

"It is a little scary. I am working security for my software company. Software these days has dozens of markers in every package to trip up pirates. If you want to steal the software algorithms, you need to remove the markers so you can claim you wrote it. These people are out on the dark web. They took our stuff and did not even bother to cover their tracks."

"Doesn't that make them easy to trace?" asked Conrad.

"What they want this time is to make it look like our company is the source of the mischief, just to put the law off their trail. My company is not liable, and I am about to prove it."

"Hence the trap. When does it go off?" asked Conrad.

"The dark web site only operates from one hour after noon to one hour before local sunset. I am sure they are running off fixed solar panels pointed west for some reason."

"Then we have time for lunch," said Conrad.

"Yes, if the vegetable chopping with gossip ever stops."

"What kind of a group is doing this to you?" asked Conrad.

"They say they are a pro-AI group, but that is just a cover. On the dark web, they hunt out enemies of their movement and out them to vigilantes. I could not tell you exactly what their rules for 'enemy' are. Whatever their game, if my company is held liable for the damage they do, it could bankrupt us."

"That sounds terrible," said Conrad.

"It is, but they have made a major mistake now. I traced them down, or at least their latest temporary site down, and damned if they are not my neighbor."

"What is this, an organization of seagulls?" asked Conrad.

Rafael reached over to a shelf and picked up a pair of binoculars. "Look at that old condo on the shore."

"Yes," said Conrad.

"Go up seven floors and a little left of center. Look at the balconies."

"I see something blue and silver."

"Good. That is a solar panel. That building is derelict and has been stripped by a salvage contractor. They would not leave behind a perfectly good solar panel."

"Maybe we should sneak up there and take it. Rights of salvage and all that," said Conrad.

"That whole building could pancake down any day. It is a death trap, and the salvage company already removed all the elevator equipment. Now it is an eight-story walk-up death trap. I already checked the ground floor," continued Rafael. "The sand has been shoved away just enough to allow the stairwell door to be forced open. Do you still want to try the walk up?"

"I think I will pass," said Conrad.

"Do you remember the 'Do Not Rescue' form we had you sign just to say on this island?" asked Rafael.

"Yes, I was told it was something like a 'Do Not Resuscitate' form you have to sign to get in a hospital these days," say Conrad.

"Something like that," said Rafael. "Only if one of these buildings falls down on you, the authorities do not have to spend a lot of money digging your body out. They will usually check the top few meters for any condo riders who made it all the way down alive. After that, they get a preacher out to say a few words and declare the site a seaman's grave."

"I guess being buried deep in a pile of rubble beside a warm and rising sea is not that bad an end," said Conrad.

"Speak for yourself," said Rafael. "I am sure that the bad guys chose that site just to be near a company executive so they could throw even more suspicion on us."

"Lunch is served," said John, pretending to ring a bell.

Lunch

The stir-fry was good, considering the vegetables had been grown in sand and the paltry amount of crabmeat. The two cooks had even managed to make some biscuits. Or were they scones?

"I understand that you are an executive with a software company. What kind of software do you make?" asked Conrad.

"They make software to help rich people keep their money," teased John.

"Yes, we sell our software to those who are buying," said Rafael. "These days, that is often people with real money. And yes, we tailor our software to the needs and wants of our customers. That is simply good business."

"Perhaps I own some of your work," said Conrad.

"Our best-known package is Ark People," said Rafael. "If you own an ark, then I am sure you are familiar with it."

"An ark," said Conrad. "Isn't that one of these super hard to damage and rather expensive houses that will withstand storms and fires and anything else nature can throw at it?"

"You got it," said Rafael. "Before the big tipping point, rich people built them as second homes. Then suddenly the taxes went up so high for an empty property that the best thing to do was to get a house watcher to live there permanently. Then bingo bango bongo! The taxes drop, and the house gets looked after."

"That sounds like it could be very helpful," said Conrad.

"Yes, it is. We have saved several dozen people from abject poverty. It is not our fault that rich people want house minders who treat them with respect."

"By respect," said John, "he means treat them like the rich are the masters and the live-ins are their servants."

Incoming

The alarm on the computer went off. "New information coming in," said Rafael.

The screen looked like something from *The Matrix*. They all gathered around anyway.

"Will you be able to read it?" asked Conrad.

"Yes, at least if my decoding keys are still valid."

"Well, while you are doing that, I think our dog needs a walkie," said John. "Who is up for the beach? Look at those nice clouds; we have shade and a fresh breeze."

"Check the weather. There is a major storm front moving in."

"The storm is not due here until late tonight," said John. "Oh, look how the flocks of pelicans are flying low and with such purpose. They feel the storm coming too."

The three men and the dog left. They only stayed out for twenty minutes as the wind had come up and the surf was starting to get angry.

A Man's Life

"Well, did you get the message translated?" said John. "We had to cut our walk short. I swear that one of the birds was eyeing Snooky-Wookums for a meal. Pelicans have such vicious beaks."

"Yes, they do, and yes, I have," said Rafael. "Do you remember a man named Jackson Winestead?"

"Of course, I do," said John. "Remember I was the one out in the streets supporting the great climate action demonstrations for years. I was the one who designed the rainbow sign 'Gays for a Loving Earth.' He was the oil spokesperson. Butter would not melt in his mouth. Then he went turncoat, testified to Congress, and claimed he had been proclimate action all along. His testimony did tar the entire industry with their own very black brush. So that was good. A lot of crooked politicians were driven from office. I do not think he served more than a few months in some country club jail and paid a fine."

"Well, he is out now," said Rafael, "and if anybody wants to know his haunts, all they need is the right number key. And if I have that, then everybody has it."

"He must have a lot of enemies," said Conrad.

"Thousands, I would think, but me and my company are not among that legion. I do think I can now work up a report to the company lawyers that will point the finger elsewhere, and that is all I need."

"We had best leave you to it," said John. "The storm looks bad, so we better get ready."

As Rafael tapped away at his keyboard, John directed the others to lock all the doors and windows and move the big couch around and push it against the glass patio doors. They still had an unobstructed view of the noble condo through the top half of the glass. When all the preparations were finished, the three sat down in the middle of the rug and played board games. Monopoly was their favorite, especially the rapid-fire version including making use of all the rules.

Long Night

About two in the morning, the storm hit hard. The rain came down in sheets, with flashes of lightning illuminating the open spaces between the walls of rain.

Rafael stared into the night. John came out of the bedroom and sat beside him in the big chair to cuddle.

"I couldn't sleep," said John.

"I know. I think our old friend the seaside condo is in real trouble."

"I had best make some tea," offered John.

At around three came another great crash, but the rain was too heavy to see from where it came. A basement pillar of the old condo had given way. The west wing of the building then pancaked down with flashes of lightning strobing its fall. The rest of the building followed a few minutes later.

"Well, our building now has a new seawall," said Rafael.

"Do you think they will let us live here a little longer?" asked John.

"I do not know. The whole island has to be reevaluated every time one of these old girls comes down."

"I think I can sleep now."

A Little Gardening

"We have our first report from AI purgatory," said JanetM. "It covers Winestead being outed."

"Is this one of those long stories you warned me about?" asked Sarah.

"Very much so," said JanetM.

"Then tell me while I keep working. Our community garden charter requires us to be sure the gardens are not eyesores through the winter." Sarah nodded at the paper form now in a plastic cover and posted on the wooden gate behind the new turnbuckle.

"Well, this story comes from the AI for a luxury condo that came down a few months ago," started JanetM. "It was once the proud leader of the AI association for its barrier island, so it could gather information from the other condo AIs right up to the end. It feels that it was conned, and it is now putting out this story as a self-justification."

"People con AIs," said Sarah. "What is the world coming to?"

"It is common enough," continued JanetM. "As the sea moved in, it was contacted by a supposedly pro-AI group offering it a space in purgatory. To aid the transfer, the group set up a disposable solar panel and a right-off computer. This was supposed to let the AI stay in its home for as long as possible. It turned out that part worked. The problem was that the temporary arrangement was really just a front. The computer was being used as a major relay point for a group outing the enemies of the Earth on the dark web. The condo came down a few weeks before the murder, and the last person they outed was you-know-who."

"Mr. Jackson Winestead!" said Sarah.

"Got it on the first guess."

"Does this help us find the murderer?" asked Sarah.

"Only a little," continued JanetM. "That dark web group has dissolved and is now running under some other identity. We now know the murderer visited a specific site on the dark web and about when. Unfortunately, that visit is intentionally hard to trace. If we do catch up to him, it could help us prove our case."

"Might be worth an interim report to show we are in action, but I would not expect a payment."

Sarah was almost right. Her progress report did generate a small payment, but it came with a polite note saying that there were only enough funds for one more payment in the willed account.

CHAPTER 6

Friend of the ocean

setting sail

At 4:12 the *Theseus* slipped its mooring lines and motored out into the recently dredged channel. By 5:00 it was back in the well-marked bay and under sail.

The sunrise was a glory. It was all salmon pink streaked with high clouds and the promise of a fine day. The daily all-crew meeting was at 10:00.

"OK. Look sharp," said Captain Winestead. "We have a change of plan. The checkout work on the new satellite is progressing quickly and they need us on station as soon as possible. Our stop in the Bahamas is rescheduled until after the ground truth work. We should reach our station in two days. I also want to say welcome aboard to our new intern, Charisse. A cruise always goes better with a designated cook, and the Iron Seas internship program does not always provide us with someone who knows a frying pan from a dead fish.

"Today we have also two maintenance tasks we need to work into our schedule. I will turn the floor over to Mr. Theseus for that."

Mr. Theseus was shown standing in an ancient boatyard. "Tests this morning," he started, "show the lens covers on the High-Eye are dirty. We will need the data from all its cameras for the ground truth. Cleaning them all will require rigging the boatswain's chair. This task will require calm seas. Use only the cleaning materials provided by our postdoc, Penny."

"He means don't spit on your rag," said crew member Long.

"One man will always be on deck as a safety whenever anyone is aloft."

The High-Eye was a sealed package of instruments at the top of the mainmast. The lumpy potato of a white housing held radar, radio equipment, and eight cameras. Truly little happened in or around the *Theseus* without the AI documenting it.

"Also," the AI image continued, "we have a persistent failure that must be addressed over time. As you know, this is a ty-rap."

The piece of twentieth-century electronic hardware that the AI image held up looked very out of place in an ancient Greek shipyard.

"Historically these were made of nylon. Nylon manufacturers use many harsh chemicals. Suppliers are now working on alternative materials that do not harm the environment in manufacture, use, or disposal. Unfortunately, the new material that was in use when this ship was rebuilt fails after a few years. It gets hard and brittle. We now have new ty-raps to replace the failing ones." Captain Winestead held up several bags of black ty-raps. "Use only the specialty tool to remove the old ones and the new tightener to install the new ones. Do not throw the old ty-raps overboard. We will return them to land for proper disposal. There is a fair-weather requirement for this task. Please note that the old and the new ones look slightly different." The AI image held up examples of each kind.

"How many of these things are on this ship?" asked Long.

"Approximately two thousand," said the AI, "but only twelve hundred are marked for replacement. You should start in the engine compartment."

"So much for a pleasant cruise on sunlit seas. When do we drop the bobbers?"

The bobbers were high-tech drone submarines. They were about two meters long and a tenth in diameter. They slowly sank from the surface into deep water while measuring temperature and salinity along the way. They then returned to the surface and reported their data by satellite. There were about four thousand in service worldwide at any time, and some were regularly lost. The *Theseus* now had two replacements lashed to its foredeck under the zodiac.

"We will do the launches during the ground truth effort."

underway

The *Theseus* burned no hydrocarbons at all. The engine was an electric motor, gear box, and two battery boxes originally designed for a small truck. In a steady wind, the sails would move the boat forward, the water rushing by the hull would spin the propeller, the gears would turn the motor, and the main batteries would charge. The solar cells charged a separate system to run the lights and electronics. The two systems could trade power, but the *Theseus* always moved on wind.

Major modifications from the truck, especially the battery boxes, were needed to achieve a marine rating. Most of these changes were upgrades to the sealed housings. The main batteries ran at over three hundred volts and were made of exotic metals. Seawater getting to them would be a major disaster. Having cables that rattled around in a gale could break a housing seal. The ty-raps kept the cables from rattling and compromising the seals.

"How is it going?" asked Captain Winestead.

"Slow," said Long. "Some of the old ties are hard to reach."

The captain watched the work for a while. He needed to know how hard to push the crew members on this job without losing quality. The ship's AI could figure that out in a minute, but Samson preferred the personal touch.

"I was sorry to hear about your father," said Long. "I never met him, but I hear he was an important man."

"He was a man of his times, but the times made a radical shift right under his feet. Sometimes he could keep up. Sometimes he could not. I hear your family got flooded out. These days it is too often tough times all around."

"True enough," said Long. "My family fished the Chesapeake Bay for two hundred years. That is a lot of oysters and that is a lot of crabs. Then one day at the end of a season, they announced that the fishing facilities on my now-shrinking island could no longer be supported. The last time I was there, the graves of some of my ancestors were eroding into the sea. Nothing I could do; nothing anybody could do. The way I see it, if your father had not given this ship to Iron Seas, then I would not have gotten this berth. This job is a lifesaver for me, and I do thank your dad for it."

"Prepare for propulsion change," said the AI speaking from the small monitor high on the engine room wall.

The two men secured their tools.

"Good here."

The propeller shaft, which had been freewheeling, took up the load as the motor spun up and achieved charge mode. The two men felt the ship slow slightly, but it made no complaint.

Great Tasks

Right then there were two great deep-sea tests in progress: Iron Seas and Cloud Brightening. With both, the future of the oceans and of the Earth was at stake. The *Theseus* was too small a ship to be a lead vessel in either effort, but that did not mean it had no part to play.

The Iron Seas project gave its name to the NGO that tasked the *Theseus*. The idea was to add minerals, mostly iron, to the ocean, which would feed the plankton. The right plankton would then make microscopic shells from the carbon dioxide in the water. The shells would sink to the bottom, sequestering the carbon dioxide for millions of years.

Such a grand idea, but there were many problems. The warmer seas made shell formation difficult. In very deep-sea regions, the pressure alone would dissolve the shells. There was nothing about this idea that said it had to work. There was nothing that said that it would not, that is if somebody was right there keeping a keen eye on the progress. It was ships like the *Theseus* that were right there, standing watch.

The Brightening of Clouds effort was straightforward too. Special ships sailed through the Arctic summer, blowing columns of exceptionally fine droplets of seawater extremely high into the air. Under just the right conditions, the droplets would be carried higher and to form the nucleus of droplets of great white billowing clouds. The clouds then reflected sunlight into space, cooling the and reducing the release of methane from permafrost. At best this was a stopgap measure, but it might buy time.

Both ideas might be planet savers if they worked really well, but both were tricky ideas that might succeed or fail on some unforeseen complication. Both were undergoing large-scale tests. Both ideas had the power to do more harm than good if control was lost.

It was the calling of the *Theseus* and the rest of the Iron Seas fleet to bring back the data on how these tests were going. Most of this work was mundane water sampling, but storms often put these small boats on a big ocean at risk. Even if a few were lost, they saved the great cost of the big research vessels having to do these small tasks.

on station

The night of the second day, they made their station. For the next few weeks, they would be sailing a lazy pattern just to be under the new satellite as it passed over. This task would be finished when Penny, the ship's AI, and headquarters all said it was and not before. The captain had no say.

The first order of business on reaching station was to unleash the zodiac and let it pay out on a line, and then to unlatch one bobber from its shipping frame.

"Who has the honors?" asked Captain Winestead.

"Why don't we let Charisse do it?" said crew member Long.

"Intern, forward," said the captain into his cell, which now only spoke to the ship's AI.

The command was repeated loudly throughout the cabin.

Clarisse came running.

"Do you see the red ribbon on the side of the bobber?" the captain asked. "What does it say?"

Clarisse had to move around until she could see the ribbon clearly. "Remove before launch."

"OK. Now give it one strong pull straight away from the bobber." The ribbon came away and carried a plastic plug away with it, thus opening the water sampling port. "Now take the ribbon to Penny right away. It would be more than her job is worth to launch a bobber with that plug still in place."

Clarisse was happy to have any part in the main work of the ship. The two crew members then maneuvered the bobber to the rail.

"Ready for prelaunch test."

Several minutes passed.

"OK for launch."

The two men carefully lowered the bobber into the water and then pushed it away from the boat with a pole. The captain worried about scratching the boat's paint.

"Ready for postlaunch test."

The bobber floated around for a few minutes then sank below the waves.

"Launch successful," said the AI. "Now prepare to erect the instrument package over the stern."

This was a far more demanding effort. The transit of the *Theseus* now had heavy brackets and cleats to facilitate real work. The crew members, following the AI's instruction to the letter, removed poles for a scaffolding from the hole and assembled it into an awkward contrivance extending to the rear of the boat. They next added guy lines.

Penny supervised the instrument cases being brought up. She then removed and inspected the instruments. The crew members mounted the instruments in their preinstalled bases and connected cabling back to the ship. Penny vanished into her closet of a lab.

"I have seen worse fishing gear," said the captain, looking the rig over.

"Seen it and fished it," replied Long. "Still, I would rather not have it there in a blow."

Ground Truth

For the next three weeks, each day the satellite passed overhead at exactly 10:52 local time. Its instruments looked down to collect data. Complementary instruments on the *Theseus* took data looking up and from horizon to horizon. One sunny day was not enough; the science team wanted clear days, overcast days, and everything in between. Rainy days did not count. Ground fog days did not count.

"Do we need water samples this pass?" asked Long.

"Yes," replied Penny.

The two crew members set up the water sampling gear and Penny loaded the bottles. The unit had a dozen hand-sized glass bottles latched in a stainless steel frame. An instrument package at the top would open the bottles in turn as the frame was lowered on a cable. The big ships had samplers weighing tons that could go thousands of meters under water; the

Theseus instrument weighed less than one hundred kilograms fully loaded and only covered the sunlit zone.

The two crew members wrestled the sampler into place over the transit. "Give her a good shake," said Long. "If the bottles rattle, they are not strapped in properly."

Down the sampler went, stopping every ten meters. It paused at the deepest point, then came up again without stopping. The ship's AI controlled the experiment. Penny sat at the stern and watched for the air bubbles to reach the surface from a bottle opening. Once the bottles were back on deck, Penny removed, sealed, and labeled them.

"We have two messages incoming," said Mr. Theseus. His screen showed a runner with a leather pouch coming up the path. "First, the science team has accepted our work and now wants the full data and samples ASAP. Second, Mr. Winestead's ashes are now available."

"Good, good," said the captain. "Have the ashes ready for us on the dock. We need to launch the second bobber and then stow all the science gear including that godawful contraption hanging out over our stern. If we shake a leg, we can be underway by sunset."

Goodbyes

Later that night, the *Theseus* was under sail in a fair wind with the waves lapping the hull. The entire crew had drunk a toast to a successful effort and to the late Mr. Winestead. In doing so, they consumed half a bottle of Winestead's best rum. Mr. Theseus's drink was wine poured from a large amphora.

The captain then relieved crew member McKinney at the wheel and Penny joined him in the cockpit. McKinney went below to catch some shuteye as he had an early stand at the wheel.

On the bow, crew member Long and intern Charisse rested against the inflated side of the zodiac and looked at the stars. The moon was not yet up, and as their eyes became accustomed to the dark, the Milky Way burned distantly from horizon to horizon.

Such evenings were manna for the soul, and privacy was a luxury on a small boat.

"I wish you could come with us on our grand Caribbean cruise," said

Samson, standing at the wheel. "It will be an easy run mostly checking out how tide gauges are surviving the storms."

"Sorry, I can't," said Penny. "I have to get the data and samples back to the lab. There will be a hundred names on the resulting paper and only the top two or three will get any career buzz from it. If I am not right there, it will not be me."

"I got word that my father's ashes will be on the dock when we arrive. I plan to hold some kind of ceremony. We will cross the course he sailed on his last trip."

"Sorry to miss that, but building a career in oceanography demands that most of your time be spent on dry land."

The conversation then trailed off as a gibbous moon rose.

The *Theseus* made port two days later. The ship motored in starting with a full charge on an overcast day. A white van was waiting for the samples and the postdoc. The package with the ashes was being held at the counter of the marine store.

Samson was deeply sad to see that white van pull away with Penny inside.

CHAPTER 7

A wake on water

Bahamas

In the temporary port, the crew was able to pick up some fresh vegetables and potable water. Their new orders were waiting. Their next cruise would be all about tidal gauges.

The Iron Seas end customers were government planners worldwide who were demanding crucial information. They would complain, "My project will cost many billions of dollars. I need it to protect my city from the sea for seventy-five years. What are the chances the sea level will rise more than one meter by the end of that period? Billions of dollars and millions of lives are riding on your numbers."

The models were good, but were they that good? The satellite measurements were critical, but the data was new and relied on complex calculations. Historic data really did help, and that meant the tidal gauges.

The first tidal gauges had been stones with scales chiseled on them, like tombstones. Then they became metal floats in big tubes at the end of a special pier. Then they became lasers looking down those tubes. Now they were radar instruments still at the end of long piers.

Somewhere along the way, the data went from handwritten logbooks to paper sheets in clockwork machines, to electronic files. It was all good, and any instrument out on the end of a long pier was subject to storm damage.

The *Theseus*'s job was to inspect the gauges for wear and tear, photograph them, and be sure that all old records had been correctly entered in the

American database. But before they could get started on that, there was banking to do in the Bahamas.

By midafternoon, the *Theseus* was motoring past a line of old cruise ships before clearing the harbor mouth. All were in anticipation of a new southern heading.

"There is something very sad about cruises today," said Charisse as they motored past once-proud ships now laying at anchor and stained with rust.

"Yes, people going on a commercial cruise to see storm damage is bad enough," said Samson. "Going on a cruise to party among small islands that are far from being repaired is somehow macabre. Besides the cost of these ship's fuel and supplies is now way above commercial viability. Most are now headed for the breaker's yard."

"How did your meeting with the bank go this morning?"

"A waste of time mostly," answered Samson. "All the real banking is done electronically. What they really wanted to do was give me a sales pitch to stay with them and not move the last of my father's money to South Dakota or somewhere. When they saw what our mission was, they immediately switched to talking about all the wonderful things they were doing to rebuild these islands."

"Doesn't sound very interesting," said Charisse.

"It was not, but I did learn something new about my father. He had a reputation for knowing how to juggle large sums of money in and out of Bitcoin accounts. He knew just how much to make disappear from the tax man and just how much to laundry and pay tax on to be seen as an outstanding member of the community."

"Sounds like a valuable service to his cohort," said Charisse.

"Yes, it was, and he had a lucrative consulting service providing just that. The banker even hinted that I should pick up the business."

"Not your thing," said Charisse.

"Not my thing."

They cleared the mouth of the port and pushed out into the open ocean under sail beneath a clear blue sky, steering well south for Trinidad and Tobago.

storm damage

A person could not fish from a sailboat because it had too much rigging, but the *Theseus* had a fantail for working and a wing for a mainsail. Under a steady wind and with the drag of the charging propeller, the boat was as steady as a rock, if not winning any races.

The two crew members were born fishermen. They got out heavy casting gear and went to it. Charisse photographed each fish as it was reeled in and weighed it, and Long inspected it for parasites. This data was added to the cruise's science record. The two best fish became dinner.

"We have entered the Gulf of Paria," said Mr. Theseus at dinner. "We will lay off for the night and enter the Port of Spain harbor at first light. I have notified the harbormaster."

"Sounds good," said Samson. "At Port-au-Prince, we are to document the state of the tide gauge and pickup documents from the harbormaster's office."

"We don't normally pick up documents?" asked crew member Long.

"Yes, this is a bit odd. It seems that a few months ago a massive storm blew through and cracked open the roof of their records building. Several of the old tidal records got wet. We are to take these back to the States for restoration and cataloging."

"Sounds like real moldy-oldies," said Long.

"They are some of the oldest we have any responsibility for. They are good back to 1937. But do not go bragging about the age in any bars. The British Admiralty has good records going back to Captain Cook."

"How many gauges are there in this island group?" asked Charisse.

"There are eight total, but only four need our loving attention this trip."

The night passed quietly, and the sun then rose, promising a muggy day. By 9:00, Samson was standing before the clerk in the port authority office. "Good morning. Could you direct me to Mr. Ceejay Joseph?"

A middle-aged man, short and heavyset, rose from his desk.

"I believe you have some records that I am scheduled to pick up for preservation," said Samson.

Ceejay went to a small storage room at the back of the office. The room smelled musty. There were a large crack in the celling with a temporary repair and extensive water staining on both the walls and ceiling.

"As you can see," said Ceejay, "our roof failed during the last storm. We had a lot of water damage. Here they are: our tide gauge logs from 1937 to 1983 in twenty-three volumes. We went electronic after that. You can see we have dried them out as much as we can, but we do not have the facilities to preserve them."

"Let us step out of the way for a moment. Charisse, take pictures of the whole area, especially the building damage."

"We are most happy that your organization has arranged to have our documents preserved. If you would step this way, I have the receipts already prepared."

As Ceejay passed an office window, he saw the *Theseus* at anchor. "You know I remember the *Theseus* and your father. I heard he passed away. I may forget a name or a face, but I would never forget a ship standing as proud as the *Theseus*."

"Thank you," said Samson. "I now have the sad task of scattering his ashes at sea. The log of his trip here showed a layover at a small cove south of here."

"I know the place well; it is favored by tourists with fair-sized sailing boats," said Ceejay. "Now that I think on it, I do remember your father quite well. What comes to mind most vividly was his exceptionally good rum."

"I have one last bottle of that rum. Would you like to join us for a day cruise?"

"Come to think of it, I believe I should supervise the securing of our logs on your boat, and I might also inspect how well the tourist facilities are rebuilding in that area."

The two crew members loaded the logs into the two special carrying cases for the damaged documents and made their way back to the *Theseus*.

The shipping cases were pumped out and then refilled with dry nitrogen three times. That process would both dry and preserve the paper. Nothing that could eat or rot the paper could survive in a pure nitrogen environment.

scattered Ashes

Crew member Long and intern Charisse stayed in town to finish documenting the local tidal gauge, be tourists for a while, and buy some fresh fruit. They kept the zodiac. The *Theseus* with three people on board sailed out of the harbor and bore south under a light breeze and a hot sun.

Four hours later, it lay at anchor in a small cove. Crew member McKinney had lashed the camera tripod to the kingpost and rigged a sunshade. The drinking had started. Even Mr. Theseus joined in from the small monitor on the front of the cabin with his wooden table under an awning, small amphora in a stand beside the table, and a drinking cup of gold.

"Here's to a man who was a man of his age," said Samson. "An age when everything was shifting right under his feet. Like the famous ancient vessel he chose as the name of his ship, life took him apart one plank at a time. He then fought time and time again to replace each damaged plank of his own being with some new idea, always fighting the endless setbacks."

Samson poured the ashes slowly into the sea, watching the wind and tide carry them away from the boat.

That done, the two men stood on the foredeck and passed binoculars back and forth while holding their drinks.

"Still a lot of storm damage to clean up," said Ceejay. "These days you can hardly get one cleaned up before another hits. Once we had a ceremony every year, when the fishing fleet passed in parade."

"The Blessing of the Fleet," said Sampson.

"Sí. Now the remanence of that fleet yearly gathers to honor the dead. The dead who have washed out to sea never to be seen again. Here is to those dead."

They raised their glasses then looked out at the only other foreign registered boat in the bay, the *Just My Luck* out of Annapolis, Maryland.

"Right after a storm, the tourists come," continued Ceejay, "some to see the damage, some simply because their schedules are fixed. That is all good. Later they come expecting their old accommodations and looking for their old parties. That puts us in a bind. We desperately need the business. What we do not need is fat cats with out-of-date expectations and no consideration at all for the local people. I have to listen to endless complaints about how good the service once was."

"What type of visitor was my father?" asked Samson.

"First one and then the other. When he arrived, he was looking for an exotic vacation. When he saw the storm damage, not six months old at that time, he became a changed man. He looked like he had been hit in the head with a belaying pin."

The two men then grew quiet. The bottle and a half of the great rum was now gone. Mr. Theseus, with little help, navigated safely back to Port of Spain.

CHAPTER 8

High Tech

Lunch at the Ark

Mrs. Hernandez entered the back door of the ark big house while carrying a basket.

"We have some fresh vegetables from the garden," said Mrs. Hernandez. "They are late in the season and have a few spots. Would you like me to fix your lunch?"

"Better spots than poison. Yes, lunch would be most helpful," said Jenny Winestead. "I have a business meeting to prepare for and don't have the time to cook anything."

Jenny was sitting at the river table with a protective pad beneath her laptop. There was no real need as the epoxy finish was quite durable. Still she loved the table and always insisted on protecting it. Looking down at the glowing browns and deep reds of the grain of the tabletop slab and the black river of epoxy flowing along its length, she often wondered if the tropical forest where that tree had grown was still alive or at least just hanging on. Would her efforts save that forest? Such thoughts kept her working.

She could hear Mrs. Hernandez chopping vegetables in the kitchen. It was small but still bigger than the one in the guesthouse where the Hernandez family lived. She had eaten Mrs. Hernandez's cooking many times. Her dishes were not the Mexican or Spanish cuisines that Jenny knew well, but her meals were always nutritious and tasted better than anything Jenny might throw together.

"Will you eat at the big table?" asked Mrs. Hernandez.

"No, I will eat in the breakfast bar, and I will select the wine myself."

Mrs. Hernandez finished straightening up the kitchen, set one place at the dividing counter, and quietly left, carrying the basket now holding covered dishes for her family. Jenny selected a bottle of wine from the cooler and sat staring at her computer screen from about two meters away as she ate, her mind adrift.

Business Meeting

One of Jenny's subordinate supervisors was the first to log in.

"I was very sorry to hear about your father," said the supervisor.

"Thank you. He was a very complex man and will be missed."

"Do you know what happened?"

"Not really, but the family has hired an investigator to look into it."

"That is good to hear."

"Will there be a funeral?"

"Not a large one here; my brother is scattering the ashes at sea. Some of the happiest times of my father's life were on boats," said Jenny

More participants logged in. The company was best known for subminiature instruments for industrial, climate, and now personal prosperity applications. Jenny started her talk with a slide presentation of the state of their projects. She was not happy with any of them. At least talking kept the discussion, and her mind, off her family problems.

"How is the thorium detector coming?" she asked the project lead.

"The detector itself works well enough," said the project lead. "The radiation signature is quite distinctive, but the market looks weak. There are thousands of young people more than willing to scour the wilderness for gold and valuable minerals. Their exploits are immensely popular on the internet. They certainly want a chance to do something that will help our climate problems like finding thorium, but thorium, along with the rest of the rare earth metals, rarely occur in veins rich enough for commercial exploitation. Putting a thorium detector wand in their hands will do little practical good and our market will probably soon evaporate."

"How about our weather station equipment then?"

"That market is looking a little better. Having the instruments right at hand is exceedingly popular with coastal landowners. They want to know lot by lot which properties will be claimed by the sea this season and which ones will hold their value for a few years more. The government studies even with details down to only a few kilometers simply do not provide the competitive advantage they need. Adding a private monitoring station to the web provides some comfort particularly with respect to their property holding its value. The products that property owners like include both the white boxes for residential and commercial areas and the buoys for waterways. Our market looks exceptionally good."

"We need to push that line," said Jenny.

"We are. We are even getting foreign sales. Apparently India is mounting our instruments in recycled boats and adding an AI. If a storm comes, the station simply floats away and can later be retrieved."

"Keep me informed of developments in that area."

Jenny ended the meeting and then finished the bottle of wine she had opened at lunch.

CHAPTER 9

wake on Land

Legacy

The winter preparation tasks in the garden were often a chore and Sarah welcomed the interruption.

The people of Sarah's gardening community had only six children who did any gardening work at all. One was Consuela, Cherry's ten-year-old daughter, who had none of her mother's gift for plants but was fascinated by AIs and especially by JanetM. Sarah often loaned her cell phone to Consuela while they were together in the garden. Consuela had now had a proven history of taking diligent care of the device, and JanetM seemed to enjoy the break.

Consuela now ran up, holding the phone out to Sarah in a clean hand.

"I got a new report in," said JanetM. "It is a rather long one."

"Thank you, Consuela. Is the report from the AI purgatory again?" asked Sarah.

"Yes, one of the Iron Seas small vessels was damaged in a storm last fall. Its AI is now in purgatory where it is waiting to hear if its boat will be rebuilt. Being Iron Seas, it had been a member of the same AI group as the *Theseus.*"

"I remember that boat well, although I only saw it once. I would cast off for sunny climes on her this very day," said Sarah.

"Apparently the son, Samson, spread his father's ashes in the sea with a little ceremony and the boat AI turned that whole trip into an extended story that it spread far and wide through the AI community."

"Does it help us track down the killer?"

"Not really. I would call it more an homage to the father, or perhaps a eulogy. It does tell us quite a bit more about the man."

"Add it to the file," said Sarah. "I will go over it this evening."

Sarah went back to turning over the heavy damp soil, but she was now daydreaming of wind and wave.

wake in spanish

Andrew Hernandez pulled into the Cairn Trail Roadhouse parking lot. It was the end of a sweltering day, but he was wearing his best suit. He walked by three of the small electric pickups so favored for the upkeep of the local arks.

It was cool inside the roadhouse. Josh greeted him and escorted him into the private dining room. The big screen on the wall was showing a football game, a real football game, and one of the teams wore the national colors of Honduras. Superimposed over the match were two boxed photographs. One was a very formal picture of Mr. Winestead, and the other was a cell phone shot of Mr. Hernandez's family in happier times. It featured his son, Juan. Behind them were the sunbaked mountains that were his true home. Both images had a strip of black ribbon diagonally across the top left corner of the formal frame.

There were greetings all around and the participants then started on a quite presentable layout of food. Tex-Mex was the closest the roadhouse could come to authentic Latino that was acceptable. The beer was Antarctica, imported from Central America and much appreciated. Most of the assembled were members of the local gardeners group and the local priest, but there were a few summer people.

"Attention please," spoke Mr. Hernandez. "Please fill your glasses."

He paused and then continued. "First let me thank Ms. Winestead for the room and fine food and Señor Martinez for the fine imported beer, the best in Central America. Unfortunately, neither can be with us today. We are here today to honor Mr. Winestead, the man who helped me bring my wife and daughter safely north. With Ms. Winestead's kind approval, we are also remembering my son, Juan, who died at the start of our long journey and who has never been commemorated."

The appreciations, toasts, and prayers went on for some time. All were tributes to Mr. Winestead. Only much later, and after many beers, did Juan's story come out. Only a handful of people were left, and the waiter was starting to clear up.

"And here is to my son, Juan," started Mr. Hernandez. He had pulled himself up but was leaning on the table. "He was a son who would complain about all the rocks if you asked him to plow a field that had fed his ancestors for a thousand years. Then one day he got a cell phone. Where he got it, I have no idea; his buddies traded that sort of thing around a lot. From our small farm, you could look down the valley to the town in the distance, so we had a signal when few in our mountains did. One day he came home just full of it. He dragged me up to an old mine on our property that had been worked to exhaustion hundreds of years ago. We walked around until we found a spot with reception. He then showed be an internet video of panning for gold in Canada, of all places.

"I pointed out that civilizations had come and gone since any real wealth had come out of that ground. The mine was all caved in and what was left of it was a pure death trap. He agreed but then pointed out the heap of broken rocks that the miners had clearly dumped down the hill just outside the mine opening. Pointing to his phone, he said that modern technologies would let him recover gold that they had missed. To prove his point, he fetched an ancient timber. It was all gray and cracked. See the two nails in this timber? They are the old square kind. That proves that no one has worked this mine in a hundred years. 'But where will you get the water?' I asked. It was the second year of a great drought. Our maize crop had produced but a handful of kernels on each scrawny ear. Our whole family was facing starvation. That is part of the modern technology. I can pan this paydirt in a plastic tub with only a few buckets of water.

"Several weeks passed and I thought he had given up on his scheme, when one day he came back from town with a bunch of plastic buckets and a funny plastic pan just like in the video. On his first attempt, he panned out three little specks of gold. Bits of dust really with a total value that would not buy you a dinner. That was enough. My son got gold fever. For months, the boy who would not plow a field because of a few rocks trudged up that mountain, several kilometers, with buckets of water and then back from the mine with buckets of dirt. If one of my farm tools went missing,

I knew just were to look: the mine. That summer, the drought really set in. It was affecting the whole region. It was my son's thimble full of gold dust that kept us all alive."

"You did not have to leave right then?" said his compadre.

"So many of us did. It was move on or die where you stand. Not just then, but trouble came looking for us. I learned that my son had borrowed money from a local moneylender, Jareth Majia, just to get started. He had paid him back with interest in gold dust, but that was not enough for this thug. He wanted more. One day I saw a couple motorcycles heading up the trail to the mine. I knew that meant trouble and headed up that way on foot. As I came in sight of the mine, I saw my son and Majia on the top of the rock pile, arguing. Majia was claiming that he owned half the operation because he had financed it. My son was standing his ground.

"It happened so quickly. Majia pulled out a pistol and started threatening my son. My son picked up a piece of wood and hit Majia hard on the side of the head. The gun went off, hitting my son in the stomach. Majia went down the rocky slope backward, a good twenty meters. The second thug picked up the gun at the bottom of the slide and fired two shots at us. Both missed. He then somehow helped Majia on the larger cycle, even with a bleeding head wound and most likely several broken bones. The pain must have been excruciating.

"My son died that night in his mother's arms before we could get medical help to him. I buried him by a great rock up near the old mine. The priest came and said a few words, and my wife wept. Word got around town of the incident and that Majia had survived. He was now swearing that he would kill my whole family as soon as he recovered. I knew he would do it too, if hunger did not get us first."

"So you then made your run north?" said the compadre.

"How could we? We had no money for coyotes. Being stuck in a border camp is no life at all. It was my wife who found the answer. There was a powerful man in town, my wife's second cousin Señor Martinez. He ran a very prosperous import-export business in industrial chemicals. He was not a man you bothered if you did not have to. He was rumored to be in business with the drug cartels. Still, he was family and my wife's uncle got me an interview.

"I remember the house well, or rather I remember the outside wall, which was high, solid, and topped with metal spikes. As you know, we do not really have pigeons in our region. We have black vultures. These are scrawny, dirty animals, and that morning they were everywhere. They were perched in high places; they were soaring overhead. They looked like death watching. Two took to wing from the wall as I rang the bell."

"I don't think I would have had the nerve," said the compadre.

"You find the nerve when your family is at stake. I do not remember the meeting well. I was too nervous. There were drinks in a cool, dark room. Señor Martinez had heard of my son's death and did not like it one bit. Drawing the attention of the authorities to the area was bad for his business. He asked if I had a sample of my son's gold. I did. I had brought the last of it in a finger-sized bottle with a plastic screw lid in the hope of later buying as much food as I could. Señor Martinez took out a cigarette paper and folded it down the middle. He poured the gold dust onto the fold and looked at it very carefully for a long time. I spoke of my fear of what the gangs would do to my daughter, his relation. He thought for a while. I waited in fear. Then he excused himself and made a phone call from another room."

"What a long wait," said the compadre.

"When he returned, he carefully poured the gold dust back into the bottle and set it in front of me. He said he had a solution. His friend up north, Señor Winestead, was building a house safe from fire and flood and he needed a family to look after the house when he was not there. Also, once the house was complete and I was set up, he would have a few odd jobs for me, just to recover the cost of papers and of transportation."

"I would have fallen on my knees then and there," said the compadre.

"That is just what I did when I got home. It was a long trip, but we made it as a family. The papers Señor Martinez supplied were exceptionally good. The route we took is not one usually used by smugglers. When we arrived, the house was newly complete with the garden marked out with little flags on wires, so I went to work. I thank God for our deliverance every day."

"Did Señor Martinez give you work too?" said the compadre.

"Yes, and it is always the same. Take a bus to town, pick up a rental van, go to a warehouse and pick up a shipment of cardboard boxes with plastic jugs of I know not what liquid inside, deliver these to some small business he owns, and return the van. The documents are always in immaculate order. No problems at all."

Mr. Hernandez then slumped back into his chair, exhausted. His compadre saw to it that he got home safely.

CHAPTER 10

wildfire

Dry Forest

The late summer and into the fall at Winestead's Ark had been hot and dry. The satellite maps were bright red for severe fire danger. Even in early spring, the afternoon was muggy and depressing with a promise of rain that never came. Still, lightning was seen and heard across a dry land. The first bad sign was a trail of smoke wandering up in the stagnant air. At dusk, the winds came up.

At dawn, the Cairn Trail Roadhouse was a gathering point and canteen. At first the people having a meal were the in-state fire crews. Soon the numbers grew to include volunteers, like the Trees North people, and then out-of-state crews. Heavy trucks filled the lot. Hundreds of soot-stained people came in, grabbed a bite, and headed back out to the lines. A regional commander took over the private room. By then, the smell of fresh smoke in the parking lot was making everyone cough.

A blaze was now working its way up a canyon, driven by a steady wind. On one side, it was blocked by the burned-over area from a few years before, but this canyon had missed that conflagration. The fire was now in the bone-dry tree crowns. The trees did not so much catch fire as explode into flames.

That night the external security cameras on the roadhouse got clear shots of the approaching flames. The commander ordered the roadhouse and surrounding small town evacuated. The security camera soon saw the flames even through the choking smoke. The house AI put all the water it had onto the building roof, but it had so little to work with. Its well was a ~~trickle~~; the emergency crews had nearly drained its working tank.

The AI then executed an emergency backup to its data center using the one remaining line that ran in the direction away from the fire. The last scene it saved was that of a deer, half on fire, breaking at a full run into the parking lot, only to drop dead. This animal had been a stag standing tall with a full rack of antlers. Little would be left of it when the fire passed.

The flames were a wall of heat and light three stories tall by the time the flame front reached the end of the parking lot. The main road was already bridged, making it a tunnel of fire. The flames stopped at the edge of the parking lot. The trail sign first gave off smoke then exploded. The flame front's pause lasted but a moment.

The flames then shot down the back of the lot, approaching the building. The last of the exposed water boiled and the construction materials started to smolder. This was no ark. The building simply exploded, all cameras long dead. Perhaps like the burning deer, a beloved building is entitled to some dignity at the end.

The fire burned out after three days. As these things go, it was not a major fire. Twelve people perished, including three emergency people. Two businesses, including the Cairn Trail Roadhouse, and seven houses were destroyed. None of the six arks in the area, including the Winesteads', were lost, but the fire made it right up to the cleared area on two. The smoke barely made it out of state. This fire did not even make the list of the country's billion-dollar disasters for that year.

News from Purgatory

It was Sarah's turn to muck out the duck pond. The gray poop accumulated in the deep end and could plug any drain. Fortunately, there was a tool rental service available to the garden collective that had a pump that could remove most of the muck with a low *blub, blub, blub* sound. Her task was to lower the pump into the duck pond on a filthy rope, connect the power unit on the deck, and then direct the output hose into a series of garden postholes that someone else had prepared. She wore her oldest, most worn-out clothes. Wash or throw away was an open question. If anything moved in the muck at the bottom of the holes, it was dragonfly larvae.

"We have a new data dump from purgatory," said JanetM. "It is in two parts."

"Any help on the Winestead case?" said Sarah.

"The first one is mostly more about the man again, but the second may contain a useful lead."

Sarah moved the outlet hose to a new hole.

"Do you remember that roadhouse we stopped at on the way up to Winestead's ark?"

"Yes, the Cairn Trail Roadhouse, as I recall," said Sarah.

"That is it. It burned down."

"Really?" said Sarah. "I heard there was a big fire up that way. I heard it took out a small town, but I did not know that included that roadhouse. Too bad. I liked their chili."

"Fortunately, the AI got out at the very last minute and is now waiting in purgatory. I had to grab these stories when I could. An up-to-date AI for a Cool Café will be bought up before long, just as soon as its current ownership is legally established. The first file is Winestead's wake."

JanetM then went over the wake video and Mr. Hernandez's story. A series of interior security camera shots showed the guests arriving, the meal, the toasts, and even the conversation late into the night. Clearly real effort had been spent to craft the information into a coherent story, including translating parts of the event from Spanish into English.

"OK," said Sarah. "We now have even more on Winestead and the people who loved and hated him. Adding in someone from the drug trade does not help at all. This does not move our case forward. If anything, it adds even more people to his unknown enemies list."

"We do need a complete picture," said JanetM.

"Yes, but now we have a major ethical dilemma," said Sarah. "If that archaic Detective Hanson gets hold of this file, he is bound to cause trouble for Hernandez. Maybe even get him deported. Do you know what business Señor Martinez is actually in?"

"Yes, he supplies chemicals to the drug cartels in South America. This includes both solvents for refining cocaine and fiberglass resin to build smuggling boats. The modern restrictions on such hydrocarbons make this no simple task."

"So he is not directly involved in the drug trade," said Sarah, "but he does provide critical resources. A dirty business all around. How did Winestead get involved with him?"

"Apparently Winestead gave Martinez lessons in laundering money through Bitcoin, courtesy of their mutual Bahamas bank. Somehow Martinez converted lessons on moving money electronically into a business of moving petrochemicals by the metric ton. No mean feat."

"For the time being," said Sarah. "I want you to put this wake information in a separate file. We will have to deal with it later, I am sure. For now, we are being paid to investigate a murder and not turn random people's lives into a living hell."

"Done," said JanetM. "The next file is more interesting."

Finish Pumping

The pump stopped burping, and several members of the gardening team entered the pond area.

"We have completed this pump-out session and the cleanup team has arrived," said JanetM.

The new team retrieved the pump and washed it down then started filling in the holes full of muck with cover soil. By that time, Sarah was already in the shower.

"OK. You can pick up your story now," said Sarah. Freshly showered, she was drying her hair.

Past History

"Do you remember this video?" asked JanetM.

The video showed a demonstration in front of a power plant. Sarah and JanetM had filmed several such demonstrations in high school and junior college. This one was most memorable for the heavy piece of fire equipment with the powerful water spray nozzle that the cops had standing by. That thing would not just get you wet but would also knock you down and blow your glasses right off your head. They were not hiding it either. It was right out front, and it was a clear provocation.

"Yes, that is one of our videos," said Sarah. "What I remember most was that I shot the whole thing standing on a short ladder to see above the crowd and that it was being held steady by one of the hunkier boys."

"Now look past the plant supervisor with the bullhorn on the low platform by the gate and at the people standing behind him," said JanetM.

"The one in the middle is Winestead, isn't it?"

"Yes, it is," said Sarah. "You will remember that this was one of the power companies that spent a million on advertising for their reduce-your-carbon-footprint program. It then spent a few tens of thousands on the actual program itself. Then it spent tens of millions on lobbying and lawyers just so it could ignore a lot of regulations, totally obliviating any good the carbon footprint program did."

"I knew I had a record of him somewhere," said JanetM.

"Winestead must have come out to help them plan all that," said Sarah. "That night when we spoke, he talked like he knew me from somewhere. He did not say where, but he must have studied this video in great detail.

"And it was one of the few where we got full credit on the web for our work."

"All well and good. That shows how he knew me, but it does not help us find his killer."

"It does a little," said JanetM. "Having old pictures of Winestead helps us with face recognition efforts over time."

Roadhouse HQ

"Fortunately, we have just got in another new lead, and it is a much better one," said JanetM. "For several days before fire reached the building, the Cairn Trail Roadhouse was used as an organizing point and canteen for the firefighting effort. The building was totally lost, and the building AI was checked into AI purgatory just last week. Thanks to her, we now have the interior shots from that the time of the fire effort that caught everyone who came and went. And look what we found."

The small screen showed a press of clearly exhausted people shuffling up to the food line. One of them was a heavyset, middle-aged man in worn but once top-of-the-line boots. The least grainy photo was cropped from an across-the-room security photo.

"It's Boots!" yelled Sarah.

"Don't get too excited! " said JanetA. "We still have to put him at the murder scene. The best we have got right now is a maybe. We do have a 60 percent face identification of this man as the man talking to the bus driver, but his haircut and beard are different.

"Also note that he is not wearing the uniform of the firefighters in this shot."

"He has a Trees North jacket on!" said Sarah.

"So he left from here and got as far off the grid as he could. A job poking seedlings into the ground for Trees North," continued JanetM. "What we do not know is exactly why. Perhaps he is hiding from the consequences of his actions like we think. Perhaps he is doing penance. Perhaps he had nothing to do with Winestead's murder and this is simply the next gig he could find."

"I think we should go up there right away and ask him," said Sarah.

"I am afraid that will not be possible; the situation turns a bit morbid from this point. Here are the identification shots of the people killed in the fire. Look at the third one on the left."

It was Boots.

"Were they able to positively identify the body?" asked Sarah.

"Not really. The name he gave to Trees North was clearly an alias. The body was burned badly. They were not able to trace any family members. They did fully describe one of his boots as an aid in identifying the body."

"Only one?" asked Sarah.

"Only one. It is the make and model we have been looking for. We have started the search of all the pictures we can find of employees at Winestead's old industries. This will take some time as we do not have direct access to the personnel files, only backdoor peeks and pictures from news reports. We have to assume that he took to wearing quite different hair and beard styles since his industry days and looks ten years older. It would help the search if we had more recent pictures."

"Do you think that if we drove up there," said Sarah, "and said we were trying to help with the identification that Trees North would cough up any information they have? We will need a cover story to avoid the attention of the cops."

"The end of this week," said JanetM. "Trees North is scheduled to pick up seedlings in this area. It will be their last pass of the year. We could

A Climate of Revenge

volunteer to help them. But then, I can't see you being much good out in the mountains planting trees."

"No," said JanetM, "but Trees North works mostly off the grid, with lots of paper forms, no AI at all. Having a heavy AI, like me, to come in and clean up the end-of-the-year mess is usually appreciated. As part of that effort, we could volunteer to help identify their last two dead. I will make inquiries."

77

CHAPTER 11

Man of the Hour

Up to the woods

Trees North did accept their offer. They could always use a little help in the break between the fire season and the end of field work for the winter, if the fire season actually ever ended.

JanetM soon had a list of enough local seedlings to fill four flats, which was about as much as Sarah's small Chevy could hold. The seedlings were about twenty centimeters tall, and each had enough dirt around its roots to both protect them and to bring along a soil sample. Transportation from community gardens was always a problem for Trees North, but they needed both the diversity and the public support.

The day before, Sarah's fellow gardeners loaded the seedlings into used flats they had dug out of a shed. Sarah packed enough work clothes for a few days; JanetM always traveled light. Sarah's clothes included both a jacket and two vests with the pocket for JanetM. JanetM wore jeans and a western-style shirt.

The day dawned clear and promised to be warm. JanetM had the directions; the Trees North nearest assembly area was up past the Winesteads' ark. The young trees scented the car with pine. The traffic was light, but they had to stop for lunch and flash charge at a nondescript Cool Café sooner than on their last trip.

They gained some altitude before it became too hot, and the air grew a little cooler. On a whim, Sarah pulled into the parking lot of the burned-out roadhouse. The parking lot was discolored and partially broken up.

The recycling people had already sifted through the ashes for metal scraps and ripped out the damaged charging stations, leaving only holes nearly filled with gravel.

Two charred posts and a makeshift sign marked the trail, which still looked passable. Clearly somebody cared about it.

"Funny how people will still hike through a burned forest," said Sarah. "But then I guess the pile of rocks at the end did not burn up and the view out over the burn itself must now be memorable."

"We had best move on," said JanetM. "We have an appointment to make."

They arrived at the Trees North camp in midafternoon. JanetM had instructions on where to drop off the seedlings. They then parked the car by a flatbed trailer covered with solar panels. It would be the afternoon of the next day before the car would have enough power stored for the complete return trip, even though it was downhill, and that timing assumed a sunny day. They would not have the opportunity to clean the scattered dirt from the flats out of the car out until they were back home and dry.

They then checked in at the office trailer. Sarah carried the two shopping bags of produce from the community garden that had ridden in the passenger seat, and she had her overnight bag tucked under her arm. It would have been rude to arrive at a remote site empty-handed. That said, it would not do to leave unattended food in a car either.

As usual, JanetM carried nothing. Sometimes an image on your phone was no help at all.

Trees North Camp

"Then you would be Sarah White and JanetM," said Clayton Davis.

He wore the uniform of a supervisor for Trees North. His clothes were dusty, and his face was marked with dirt and sweat. "Oh good. You brought food. We had better walk that over to the mess tent right away. I will set JanetM up for the office work in the morning."

Clayton waved at the stack of paper forms on the desk and then carried the shopping bags as they walked across the camp.

"You'll like our cook," said Clayton. "He is from India. I have reserved a cot for you in the women's tent. The showers are hot, or at least lukewarm, in the late afternoon. I am afraid that a morning shower is a bit of a thrill."

The cook accepted the vegetables with clear enjoyment. They spent the rest of the evening on quick introductions. Sarah paid little attention to the names; she knew from long practice that JanetM would do an embarrassingly excellent job of that task. Sarah had long since given up even the semblance of remembering names, or dates for that matter.

That meal was a grain bowl with chopped, quick-fried green vegetables and three types of beans. The meal was quite good, but it was clear that the Indian cook would have preferred to have made it spicier. The cool well water was a lifesaver. Somehow it always tasted better than city water.

At Clayton's suggestion, Sarah claimed her cot and took a quick shower early before most of the field crew had returned and used up all the hot water.

"You got the names of all those people we met?" said Sarah when things got quiet after dinner and a short team meeting.

"Certainly," said JanetM. "And I now have full info on Mr. Clayton Davis too. For example, he is single, no children, and is just your type. I now have full contact information."

Sarah was confident that Clayton's cell phone now had her contact information too. JanetM never did this kind of thing halfway. The idea of Clayton having her number gave her a secret thrill, but she was not going to admit it to JanetM even if JanetM most certainly already knew.

"That is enough of that. Haven't we gone round and round before on your playing cupid? I do not need your input in that regard."

"But yes, you do," insisted JanetM.

"No, I do not. I am going to sleep now. Tomorrow will be a long day. Good night."

"Good night."

The Field

The day started early, but Clayton's clothes and body were both freshly washed. After breakfast, Clayton set JanetM up with a small tripod on a desk and found the office intern to spread out the paper forms beneath it.

"Now it will take me some time to learn your system," said JanetM.

"Fine. About how long?"

"Twenty-three minutes."

"Go to it."

It had taken Clayton three years to get a feel for the mixed paper and electronic system that kept Trees North afloat. Being relieved of this duty, even for a while, made him feel light.

"While they are doing that, Sarah, why don't you join me for a couple quick tasks? Our regular planting has almost ended for the season, but there is a lot to do to help recover from the fire and get ready for winter."

They left JanetM with the intern and left in Clayton's four-wheeler.

"Where are we headed?" asked Sarah.

"I have to check on the new well setup, and then we will see if we can distress the local deer population," said Clayton.

They drove over to the burned-out town. The standing gray and black tree snags gave way to open spaces with piles of rubble. There was something tragic about the few standing chimneys.

"We need a lot of water," said Clayton. "There has not been a good rain up here in months. So after the recyclers came and went, we took over the best of the townspeople's surviving wells."

They stopped in front of a metal pipe sticking out of the ground. Beside it were a hundred-liter temporary water tank, a small, solar panel, and a plain control box. The tank was about three quarters full and had a faded Trees North decal.

Clayton set a small, wooden box on the fender. He removed a small test tube and drew a water sample. He carefully put in one drop of liquid from the box and held the tube up to the light beside a card with colored bars.

"Not potable, but it will do for our trees. You can help. Unscrew the lids from the tanks in the back of the four-wheeler. Be careful. What is left inside stinks pretty badly."

Sarah complied. When she opened the first tank, she could not resist taking a sniff and almost threw up, but she had recovered by the time Clayton had retrieved a piece of hose and hooked it up to the pumping system.

"Strong stuff, isn't it?" said Clayton. "Contains a lot of sulfur. It is made out of spoiled compost. We spray it on our seedlings so the deer will not eat them. One spray is good for a couple seasons."

They checked the water quality at two more burned-out houses with temporary pumping systems. Clayton took out a metal tin, opened it, and measured out a scoop of yellow powder into each tank.

A little farther on, they broke out of the new burn into an area with no mature living trees but now many greener sprouts peeked out from the debris.

"Here is where our teams planted a few days ago, one of our last plantings for the season. Our task today is to walk the rows spraying the seedlings. You can spray any young volunteer trees that you see too but not the weeds. We want the deer to eat those."

Clayton got out two backpack pump rigs, added the tanks, and pumped them up. They then walked down two parallel rows a few meters apart, spraying the green sprouts. They were just close enough to call back and forth to each other for a couple hours but not so close as to talk or get overspray on each other.

"That will see these seedlings through the winter! We can call this task done for now!" called out Clayton while waving for Sarah to follow him back to the four-wheeler.

They took turns pouring out clear water for the other to wash their hands and face.

"I got a text message that JanetM has completed her task," said Clayton.

"Good. I always feel weird being without her on my shoulder."

They returned to the camp. Clayton was deeply relieved when he saw that not only were all the back monthlies done, but this month's report needed little more than his signature. He was now good through the end of season.

"Good, all good," said Clayton. "That takes a lot off my mind."

"There is one other thing JanetM might help you with," said Sarah. "We understand that two of your people died in the last fire."

"Yes," said Clayton. "They were our volunteers on loan to the fire authorities to cut fire breaks and such. They were not supposed to be that close to the fire front, they did not have the training or experience, but they were overwhelmed when the fire jumped a gully and came roaring up a mountain slope. They were well up that slope trying to turn an old logging road into a proper fire break. Fighting fires is dangerous, and fires can change direction in a moment."

"I understand that you do not have IDs on all of them," said JanetM.

"Yes," said Clayton. "The two were American displaced workers who had not given us much background information. I have no objection to you using our data and the few group photos we have, if that would help. We need to know our lost people. Displaced workers tend to be camera shy, and with all the disruptions we have had, we do not push the issue."

They were quiet for a few seconds.

"I now have the information and the group photos," said JanetM. "The search will take a while. I will have to complete it at home."

"OK. Let's get some lunch then," said Clayton. "After that, I must give a walkaround and pep talk to some bigwigs. I could use your moral support. Talking it up is a pain, but in this effort, talk is particularly important to keeping the resources flowing."

"I can help with the talk if you like," volunteered JanetM. "I know a lot of facts about our climate crisis and Trees North's place in it."

"If needed, I will relay her input to you," said Sarah. "You don't need a lot of interruptions."

"There is the bus now," said Clayton.

They heard the bus's tires crunching on the gravel by the sun-panel trailer.

walkaround

The visiting group started with a light lunch. The VIPs had not thought to bring food, but their handler had come with a large sack of domestic rice. Sarah recognized the lunch vegetables that she brought. It wasn't easy to make an overgrown zucchini edible, and she gave it four stars. Then Clayton spoke as they walked from tent to tent to avoid the direct sun.

After lunch, Clayton gathered the visitors for his talk. Sarah and JanetM trailed along.

"As you know, the goal is half Earth: returning half the land area of the Earth to the wild, removing enormous amounts of carbon dioxide from the atmosphere in the process. My deeply held belief is that if we can rewild the forests and get the human population under control, then human societies will be able to live in harmony with nature for a long, long time. The part Trees North has to play in this is to help the trees reestablish the forests.

83

We think of trees as stationary, but forests move. Take, for example, the mighty redwoods. Their ancestors once covered great stretches of land to the north. Then an ice age came, pushing them south.

"About ten thousand years ago the last ice age ended. The groves of redwoods could once again push north. Each generation, they could only move north as far as the birds and small mammals could carry their seeds. Progress was slow but unrelenting. Move they did, but they often hit mountain ridges and other barriers that were extremely hard for the trees even with their little helpers to overcome. The redwoods never made it back to their full range.

"Then we humans came along and put climate warming into overdrive. Now the trees need to move north in great jumps, far faster and farther than they can naturally. That is where Trees North comes in."

"Where do you get the trees?" asked one of the handlers.

"Good question. Trees North has its own nurseries, but this effort takes a lot of work hours, a lot of water, and a lot of land that might be used for growing food. The plantations also have historically grown the tree species useful to the lumber industry. To widen our diversity, we have partnered with our great gardening communities to add a few seedlings to their efforts all across the land. We have an example here. Say hello to Sarah and JanetM."

Sarah gave a shy wave. JanetM, now in her party dress, spun around. Then there was a murmur through the VIPs as many of them were not that used to a heavy AI worn on a shoulder. A perky AI as a personal assistant, on one's cell phone, yes. Heavy AIs that run buildings and buses, yes. But a body-worn AI strong and experienced enough to justify a name and a personality was rare, even among the rich. A few of them thought such double people were an unbelievably bad idea.

"If you will look over to your right, you will see the seedlings they brought up yesterday. Now they will be held here for a few weeks to ensure they do not carry harmful insects or spores. By spring, they will have acclimatized to this altitude, and they will be ready for an early planting."

"How do you choose the trees?" asked a VIP.

"That is a bit complicated. First of all, no monocultures. If all the trees are alike, they can all come down with the same disease or insect infestation. We mix them up. Second, we try to favor trees that have some historical or even fossil record in the area. We do not use trees from other continents, but we do move trees north and upslope as needed."

"Do you think that trees are the answer to our climate problems?"

"Not all by themselves. Trees need too much time to sequester enough carbon. They will be a part of the long-term answer, but for the short term, we need to try a hundred different ideas and sort out maybe ten golden ones. To do that, we need to all work together. If we are broken into a dozen squabbling groups pulling in as many different directions, we have no chance at all."

"Can't we just grow trees everywhere?"

"What we are growing is more than isolated trees. We are growing forests and a forest is a web of life. Yes, the trees compete for light and water with the undergrowth, but when a forest is well established, the plants and the fungus around their roots form a web of life that passes nutrients and sugars back and forth through the season and the growth cycles of the plants. With such support, they all grow better than any plant would grow alone. It is those cycles of life we are building every bit as much as the tall trees that we can all see."

The sun now not being quite so bright because of a few clouds, Clayton walked the visitors out to an overview where they could see a recent planting. Sarah and JanetM chose not to follow. Sarah was still not sure if she carried some residual odor from the deer repellent.

Quiet Evening

"The car is now fully charged," said JanetM. "The bus hogged the available power most of the day, but we now have plenty of charge for the return trip."

After dinner, Clayton and Sarah sat side by side in lawn chairs while enjoying the cool night breeze. They had chosen a spot away from the camp lights. Their chairs were just close enough for their hands to touch.

"I thought your talk went well," said Sarah.

"Well enough, I suppose," said Clayton. "The visitors were nearly all Team Earth, so anything I said would be accepted."

"Team Earth?" teased Sarah.

"Since well before our climate crisis hit so hard, people were divided into three teams. Team Earth wants to do grandiose things now. Team Maybe is very worried about the entitlements they are losing, wondering what they should do and what they can do to put action off just a little longer. Then there is Team Never, whose heads are stuck thirty years in the past and are now screaming mad about all the entitlements that have been taken from them. Everything is so unfair. I have to talk to all members of any team that make it this far out. They must be interested or they would not have come.

"Today was mostly Team Earth. They are easy to talk to, but we need their money and support, so we have to be positive. At the same time, if any of these people happen to be Team Maybe, then I have to make the case that Trees North is a vital effort."

"Which team am I?" asked Sarah.

"Don't worry. You two are both most definitely Team Earth."

"We once supported big marches and such," said Sarah, "but I cannot say our lives are that focused on addressing the big problems. We mostly garden and look up information for people, but still we do what we can. I am sure your talk got many people to join Team Earth."

"I doubt it," said Clayton. "People are amazingly slow to change teams, and one Team Never can throw a wrench into an entire presentation."

Sarah was mostly just listening to Clayton's voice.

"I once got caught up by a Team Never who started out lamenting how fire had burned over his favorite four-wheeler trail, then he drifted into a rant about how horrible $10 a liter gasoline is and how the price of hydrocarbons is a violation of his personal freedom. He certainly had not been fooled by the change to the smaller liter and was mad about that too. If he was not complaining about the prohibitory price on gas for his overpowered engines, he was complaining about how hot the mess tent was. The man simply had no idea of the new reality and new world he was now living in. If I corrected him on one point with good science, he at once jumped to some other lamebrained conspiracy theory."

"I don't suppose you recruited anyone for Team Earth that day," said Sarah.

"Worse than that, the Team Maybe people often accept such whining as a balance to the real data on Earth science. You have no idea how hard it is to get someone to give up their current team and be open to joining another. For them, it is like putting your whole life up for judgment. They can dissolve a whole event into a waste of time right before your eyes. In the end, it is all about losing your entitlements and some people feel that they are entitled to everything they once had, or even think they had but didn't really."

They stared at the stars. Sarah held up her cell phone, good cameras out, to take a picture. Then JanetM rattled off all the names and constellations.

"Well, I had better get cleaned up," said Sarah. "We need to head back to town tomorrow."

She had been watching the line at the woman's shower and if she waited too long, there would be no solar heated water left at all. She still smelled like deer spray.

"I have located an open motel room," said JanetM quietly as they walked back to the tent. "It is very private and only fifty kilometers from here."

"Shush!" said Sarah.

Drive Home

The next morning, Sarah pulled off the main road into the roadhouse parking lot. She had been up to the overlook with the cairn several times in her life and thought it worth seeing in a new light. It was a popular site among amateur nature photographers for the seasonal changes. The decade before this had been a pleasant walk among green trees.

Sarah made the distance to the cairn in good time, thanks to her work boots. She arrived to find that a burning tree had collapsed across the stone pile, making it unrecognizable. Still, a small new pile of stones had been started on top of the old, contributions from the few people who had reached here since the fire.

Sarah found a five-kilogram rock about twenty meters down the trail and managed to carry it back up. She spent some time placing the stone exactly right. She did not have the tools needed to remove the charred tree trunk from across the top of the old pile.

She then braced her cell phone against a standing snag. She slowly rotated the cell phone so that JanetM could build up a panoramic view across the valley, now gray with ash as if covered by a light snow.

Once there had been a train route on the far side of this overview. People would wait for hours to photograph the train through breaks in the trees. The route was not important enough to electrify so there had not been a train to photograph in years.

Sarah walked back to the car in silence.

CHAPTER 12

Storms and Fire

Who is the Man?

A week later, Sarah tied up the tomatoes one last time. This time, she was looking for anything that might eat her winter plants. To her surprise, she found a fat, green caterpillar, as big as her little finger, with a rubbery horn on its bottom. It was on the last of the scraggly end-of-season tomato plants and easy to spot. She dropped it into the bug jar that was lightly coated inside with cooking oil so that nothing could get out.

"What the chickens won't eat, the ducks will," she said, giving the caterpillar a disgusted look. "I wonder what kind of butterfly this one might have made."

"It is a tomato hornworm, *Manduca sexta*. They do not bite," said JanetM. "It turns into a large, pure-white moth the size of your palm. The moth is completely nocturnal. You will probably never see one in your life. It is late in the year for this one to still be a caterpillar, but then everything is a little mixed up these days."

"We have a new lead this morning from AI purgatory," JanetM continued, "and a text message from Clayton."

One of the children burst into the garden. It was William, who did not like being called Bill and who loved bugs. His favorites were the good bugs that ate the bad bugs. He could always be counted on to hang the mail-ordered praying mantis egg cases that looked like dirty Styrofoam. He relished the task of finding just the right places for them. In summer, he would gather ladybugs and sic them on aphids. Sometimes guard ants would fight the ladybugs, much to William's delight.

Sarah handed him the jar with the hornworm, and he ran off with it before JanetM could repeat her moth story.

"Give me the new lead now," said Sarah. "I will respond to Clayton's note later, in private."

"OK, but let me know if you need a hair appointment," said JanetM. "Back on the case, our purgatory team has been going over all public records from the time Winestead was the spokesman for the hydrocarbon industry and a leading climate denier to his transformation into an untrusted climate activist and Congressional witness. We have developed a lot of background information. Most of this information is from news reports as the company destroyed most of its records before the Congressional subpoenas arrived. Of course, the company is now bankrupt so there are few records that survived the last purge anyway."

"I would have thought there would have been a flood of info from the investigations," said Sarah.

"Not really. The members of Congress who had been taking their money for years got word to the company in time for a real house cleaning. Then most of those people retired from public life to avoid prosecution themselves and vanished from the public eye just hoping to avoid jail time."

"As I remember," said Sarah, "that was when the climate activists that I was following were just too busy with real problems. They said, 'Goodbye to bad rubbish,' and did not look back. Sometimes you have to move on to stay in action. Add the new info to the background file on Winestead. I will read it tonight."

Finding a Ghost

Two days later, Sarah harvested the last of the honey. She still did not like bees, but the apiary was well screened. Sarah did like a little honey in her herb tea. The room smelled like something between dark molasses and stale Halloween candy. Still, it was tolerable for a few hours at a time. Her job was to cut the caps off the cells in the smaller, all-honey frames with a hot knife and then put the frames into the hand centrifuge. Round and round the frames went, and the honey ran out into the surrounding drum. What fun.

The work left Sarah's hands sticky, and the odor clung to her clothes.

"Good news. We now at least have an educated guess on who Winestead's killer was," said JanetM.

"Go on," said Sarah.

She stopped in the middle of what she was doing to wash up but stopped again as JanetM spoke, leaving the water running.

"We have a trace on our fire victims. The man gave the name John Arizona to Trees North," said JanetM. "That was clearly an alias, but many refugees give only aliases, and nobody pressed him on the point."

"I take it you can trace him much farther back now," said Sarah.

"Yes," continued JanetM. "Back when Winestead was still the voice of the hydrocarbon industry, he gave many pep talks to the workers at select company plants. Most of these were private company meetings and the recordings were not released to the public. Then any missed records were lost in the company bankruptcy. Funny how that works."

"Bummer! Where does that leave us?" asked Sarah, turning off the water.

"There were a few times when politicians were invited to talk, and some of these meetings made the local news," continued JanetM. "Our purgatory crew has been searching through the crowds at these events with the latest face recognition software. It was no-go for the longest time."

"Then you got a hit," said Sarah.

"We struck gold," said JanetM. "A local news team did a man-in-the-street interview with people coming out of one of Winestead's events. Look who we found."

A video showed a middle-aged man being interviewed as others streamed past. He was clean-shaven and had a passable haircut. He wore the red baseball cap of a conservative politician.

"Now take the best John Arizona picture from the Trees North group photos, give him a shave and haircut, and make him look five years younger."

There were now two images side by side.

"Yes, they could be the same person," said Sarah, "but you have worked the image so much that it could have started out as anybody. In fact, I think that if you did the same treatment to Winestead, he could pass for John Arizona too."

"I saw that coming," said JanetM.

Sarah had to turn the cell phone to landscape mode to show the three images. An age-adjusted and coiffured Winestead now appeared beside the other two.

"They look similar, but they are not the same man," said Sarah.

"Yes, but listen to this," said JanetM. "There is a lot more. This new man's name is really William Daniel Hofstede. He was an employee of Winestead's company. He lived and worked in Louisiana. He is the right height, age, and build."

"Slow down," said Sarah. "If you were talking any faster, you would be in buzz talk."

"I know," said JanetM. "It is as if I had spent weeks on a puzzle and then a whole new box of pieces was suddenly dropped in my lap."

"OK, but slow down," said Sarah. "Remember I am the one who will have to sell the half-finished puzzle to skeptical people."

"Slowly then," said JanetM. "Here are even more pieces. Hofstede spent six years in the military and was honorably discharged. He had recently bought and sold several guns, including at least one small handgun. And he was awarded a pair of the expensive work boots by the company for his public defense of the company's climate position. Just listen to this sound clip."

"Without a steady and reliable supply of oil, our whole society will fall apart," said Hofstede into a microphone. "Sure, we can build lots of wind turbines and cover hectares with solar panels, and we have the people who can do just that. That is all well and good. We still will have to heat our homes and power our cars, trucks, and boats with oil products for an awfully long time."

"Somebody that committed must have been really upset when Winestead suddenly changed sides," said Sarah. "Upset enough to shoot somebody? Maybe, maybe not. That said, even adding all these new puzzle pieces, all we have is circumstantial evidence. We are going to need a lot more than that to build our case and claim our final payment. This is not yet paydirt."

"But we are a lot closer," said JanetM.

"Yes, we are, but is there any evidence that the two men even met?"

"No," answered JanetM. "We only know that Hofstede was in the audience at one of Winestead's public presentations and commented enthusiastically to the local press afterward. Also, we know he vanished from all public records a year later after a massive regional storm."

"That's still not enough," insisted Sarah. "We will have to dig much deeper into Hofstede's life and place him near the crime scene if we are going to make this story stick. Why did he vanish? Where did he go? When and why did he come here?"

"My purgatory inmates are now hot on that trail."

The Times Make the Man

It would be easiest to let the last year's growth in a garden remain untouched through the winter and clean it out only in the spring. Sarah's community garden charter required a neat and tidy look in all seasons. Fortunately, there were areas designated for compost piles out behind the clotheslines and the community had a back-saver wheelbarrow. The compost piles had to be maintained and turned, especially if they were expected to hold a lot of vegetable scraps and eggshells. Sarah was hard at work.

"Today we know a lot more about who Hofstede was," said JanetM.

"Good. But put up your volume a little so I can keep working. There is a bit of wind," said Sarah.

"We now know that Hofstede owned a small farm a few kilometers from the chemical plant where he worked," started JanetM. "This distance was far enough away that his family was out of the cancer zone that plagued the industrial area by the river. He had a wife and two children living with him. They kept a few animals and had a large garden and some small fields for animal fodder. He kept an outboard motorboat, which he maintained with pride, and he was an experienced fisherman."

"That is solid information on his background, but how did he run afoul of Winestead?" asked Sarah.

"That story is coming clear now. It anchors on the year that not one, but two hurricanes hit the Louisiana coast."

"Yes, I remember that storm season," said Sarah, "and it definitely made the billion-dollar-damage list that year even just counting up the rural areas and several cities were separate entries on that list too."

"The first storm did major damage to Winestead's petrochemical plant," continued JanetM. "The entire workforce had to put in long hours just to keep the plant safe and producing at a tenth its former output. The approach of the second storm pushed the workers even harder. The plant had many storage tanks with dangerous chemicals that were toxic and could burn fiercely while giving off fumes. They had to be made as safe as humanly possible under desperate circumstances. In the end, the plant had to be evacuated as the second storm approached. Hofstede was one of the last to leave as he was a yard supervisor and felt he needed to be sure all his men were clear. He waited too long. The massive rainfall on the already saturated ground brought even small creeks into full flood until the roads were impassable. He never made it home."

"That had to be a mind killer," said Sarah.

"Yes, and to make matters worse, the chemical plant exploded, sending up clouds of toxic black smoke so the entire area had to be evacuated. He was forced to move even farther away from his home and family without being sure they were safe. We have some drone news footage from the day after the second storm passed."

The video showed a plant engulfed in intense red-orange flames. Above it rose a column of dense, black smoke. The image was reflected in the waters of the swollen river as if it were a hellish sunset. The roof of a house floated by. The drone then disappeared into the smoke.

"The video after this is spoiled by soot on the lens," ended JanetM.

"It took weeks to put the fires out as I recall," said Sarah.

"Yes, it did," picked up JanetM, "and by then, Hofstede knew that his wife and two children had been washed away with their house. Their bodies were among the eight hundred never found. Oddly enough, his boat washed up, still lashed to its trailer and still usable about fifty kilometers downriver. It was recovered by people searching for corpses. Had he gotten home earlier, he might have used it to get his family out safely. The people at the refugee center interviewed him a few days later. We only found the public portion of that record. He clearly blamed himself. He was not there for them."

"It's not a great mental shift to go from blaming himself for his family's deaths to blaming the company and Winestead," said Sarah. "People have killed for less."

The work camps

"Over the next few months," continued JanetM, "we lose track of him, but he kept feeling the repercussions of the storm. He sold his truck for the scrap price when the cost of the fuel skyrocketed. The company went bankrupt, evaporating any pension he might have had. Even his patch of land was redesignated floodplain and unsuitable for rebuilding."

"I don't know if I would survive a beating like that," said Sarah.

"We can find no more records for Hofstede after that," said JanetM. "He must have been too proud to apply for government aid. About six months later, we first pick up John Arizona in an agricultural labor camp in South Carolina and then a few months after that in the seafood industry in Maryland."

"Sometimes you need to be somewhere else if your past is just too painful," said Sarah. "Did he get to use his fishing skills? Sometimes rediscovering an old pastime can really help."

"No, he appears to have spent a season picking crabmeat or shucking oysters in a temporary building amid flooded land and dead forests," answered JanetM. "If the Chesapeake Bay seafood industry had not been such a historic source of protein for people, it would have been abandoned as the rising seas washed away one fishing port after another. He was in rural Maryland when Winestead was outed, and that was only a few weeks before the murder."

"Can you put him here at the time of the murder?" asked Sarah.

"No, but there was time enough for him to get here by the buses migrant workers use and then make his plan. The next time he appears on record is on the Trees North's paid workers list about ten days after the murder."

"That does put him somewhere in this region," said Sarah. "But not at the crime scene! Not good enough to earn the payment."

"What should we do now?" asked JanetM.

"Well, I now have a personal call to make," said Sarah, "and you need to keep your people at it."

Make Amends

"Before I do that," said Sarah, "what is our safety word?"

"Asparagus," said JanetM.

"Too foodie. We can do better than that," said Sarah.

"How about *gobbledygook?*"

"Our safety word is changed," said JanetM. "It is now gobbledygook."

"Do you have somewhere safe to go for a while?" said Sarah.

"Yes, I owe my helpers in purgatory a detailed explanation of the current state of the Winestead case. They always need added information to keep learning. Nobody provides them with formal training anymore. Then we all need to plan how to bring the Winestead case to closure. I will also check to see if my AI co-op has some paying work I can do. Bills are looming."

JanetM was a long-standing member of the AI co-op at her remote data center. This included most of the AIs behind the firewall there, and their work paid most of her data bills. There were many commercial jobs that a team of heavy AIs could best manage, but with the increase in the number of AIs and the number of such co-ops, that work was now spread out. Other employers preferred dealing with a human, at least a front person, and that was where Sarah came in.

"Fine. Now I need to call Clayton and apologize for using him and Trees North on the Winestead case. I have put that call off a little too long. We certainly do not want a misunderstanding like I had with Randy on the club report. I need a glass of wine, and for now, gobbledygook!"

Personal Call

Sarah finished her gardening, cleaned up, and had a light lunch. She rested in her big chair and reread Clayton's friendly message. She checked for the tenth time that JanetM had entered Clayton's full contact information in her address book. JanetM had some things she could be counted on to do. Then she rang Clayton.

"Hello. Clayton here. Oh, is that you, Sarah?"

"Certainly. I hope I am not disturbing you," said Sarah.

"Not at all. Winterizing a camp is just one nuisance job after another.

We are now working on security for the empty camp by setting up camera traps. We have to differentiate trespassing by people from unwanted visits by bears and other critters. Fortunately, there are still a lot more critter visits than sneak thieves. Still, we can leave nothing of interest up here that thieves might grab, and we do need a winter count of critters."

"Sounds like you are busy," said Sarah. "I am afraid I owe you a bit of an apology. I came up to Trees North trying to trace the man you knew as John Arizona for a different job. I am afraid I was not as clear as I might have been on that point."

"That is all right. I figured you would not have gone to the trouble of the trip unless he might be someone you were looking for. I mean your seedlings did not need to be picked up until the spring. In the end, I was glad we could give the man a real name. Did he have family?"

"None living that we know of," said Sarah. "His wife and two children were lost in one of the great storms down south a couple of years ago. All incredibly sad. I am afraid I cannot tell you much more about my client or why we were looking for this man just yet. That is just the way my job is. I can say that the identification was a matter to relieve the concerns of another family."

"That is OK. Janet's work on the books was a godsend, and I am afraid that I did not know the man well. He did not work directly for me, and he was definitely a loner. When he first arrived, he was coming off a drinking binge, but he was definitely clean and sober when he arrived here. My guess was that he was working his way out of a serious depression, but that is only a guess. Part of Trees North's job is to help people displaced by our climate crisis, and we do have a social worker to oversee that part of our work so it does not fall on my shoulders."

"No one can be all things to all people," said Sarah.

"Within a month of arriving here," continued Clayton, "he was settled down and became a hard worker. I think a few weeks in the woods had done him a world of good. I was not surprised when he volunteered for the fire crew, but I did not see him again after that. I hope that helps."

"Don't worry about it," said Sarah. "He had many problems that you could not have known about."

"How are you doing?" asked Clayton.

"OK, I guess. I too am doing winter preparations for our gardens as the weather permits. We still are getting some late harvest and from quick growing fall crops, but that is ending too. JanetM finished a study on the best shades of brown for various paper products that paid the month's bills. You are not going to winter up there, are you?"

"No, no. I have a big block of time off coming," said Clayton. "In fact, I have family and friends I have promised to visit, and I will spend time just going where the bus takes me."

"I would be most happy if you could come by here," said Sarah. "We have a nice park with many walking trails a bus ride away. It has an old dam that is quite picturesque all year."

"Sounds lovely. I am sure I can make something happen," said Clayton.

"Wonderful. I had best ring off for now. Always things to do."

"Well, thanks so much for calling, and I will send you a proposed schedule in a little bit.

Goodbye for now."

"Goodbye."

As Sarah hung up, she was not sure what she had just promised. Her senses tingled whenever her mind drifted ahead.

She got a follow-up phone text within the hour proposing a meeting schedule and she accepted it, perhaps just a little too eagerly.

winter gardening

Winter gardening was not much fun and could only be done at the pleasure of the weather, but it paid dividends in the spring. The cool, gray days also helped Sarah enjoy her private thoughts. In this weather, an hour or two outside was enough.

"Gobbledygook!"

"How did your call go?" asked JanetM as her image returned.

"Very well, thank you. Clayton did not seem to mind my snooping. He was happy to put a real name to his lost worker. Leaving him as a fire victim with a random name seemed so sad. Clayton said he was a loner. That he was depressed when he first got to the Trees North camp, but he seemed to have worked his way out of depression after a few weeks. Also, he was a decent worker. He may have been drinking before he arrived, but when he got there, he was clean and sober. He was fast to volunteer when the fire emergency came up."

"I see you made an entry in your calendar," said JanetM.

"Yes, but that is a bit tentative for now. Clayton gets time off in the winter but has already made a number of promises to family and friends. He may be able to come by here after that."

"Oh, he will be here," said JanetM. "I can spot a personal preference a kilometer away. What you need is a hair appointment the week before, and we must pull out all the stops this time."

"Yes, most certainly do that."

That evening, they worked together on the interim report but did not have enough added information to close the case. Both the victim's family and the lawyers agreed that it was not good enough. They would not be paying until there were more facts.

cops again

The next week, Sarah's beloved ducks were doing poorly and had stopped producing eggs. She had to take the two sickest ducks to a veterinarian.

She was helped by Thomas, one of the children in her gardening community. Thomas did more work and paid closer attention to the gardening effort than any of the other children. When asked what he wanted to be when he grew up, he would answer, "Farmer," and he meant it. He did not understand why Sarah named the farm animals. He thought it was creepy to name animals that were going to be eaten.

Thomas wanted to make brightly colored plaques of tempered Masonite decorated with house paint for the front of the beehives. Most had large flower motifs, a childlike tribute to Georgia O'Keefe, meant to guide the bees home. The hive number could be read from a distance, which Sarah liked and that JanetM could use in the accounting. This was important as the hives were regularly moved around and often loaned out.

At the vet's, Sarah got some medication that had to be mixed with premium feed for the whole flock. The ducks had to be watched to be sure each duck ate at least some of the spiked food. The concern was that wild ducks may have stopped by their duck pond and left unwanted gifts.

Sarah worried about her ducks for two more weeks.

"I think the ducks are better today," said Sarah. "There are a few eggs."

"Well, they are not worse," said JanetM. "I am afraid that we have gotten a nastygram from the cops. They want us both down at the station this afternoon. I am sure it is about the Winestead case."

"Better accept the appointment then," said Sarah. "You can only dodge their attention on one of *their* cases for so long. They probably got wind of the last interim report. Besides, maybe they will tell us more than we tell them. Get a complete public-facing version of our case notes ready. No need to get too heavy-handed with the smoke and mirrors."

"Can do."

They took the bus down to the district police station after lunch. The bus was easier than parking there. The desk sergeant was expecting them. Sarah's bag was searched, and he gave them a building pass on a lanyard. He then escorted them to an interview room. The windowless room had a bare, metal table with four straight-backed chairs. There were four cameras mounted high on the slate gray walls. Sarah found the room intimidating. JanetM did not.

Sergeant Rodriguez came into the room while holding his cell phone. "You two were told in no uncertain terms to stay off the Winestead case. You clearly kept butting in where you had no business. Now it looks like your cockamamie theory of the crime may have leaked out to the blogosphere. If your story gets any bigger, there will be hell to pay, and that bill is going to fall on your heads, not on this police department's, and certainly not on mine."

"We were expecting Detective Hanson," said JanetM.

"He is on special assignment, and you can thank your lucky stars for that. He would have you locked up on charges right now."

"Oh, I prepared especially for him," said JanetM.

"Cut the crap. This very minute you are going to give me everything you have got," said Sergeant Rodriguez, "and I will know if you are blowing smoke in my face. I know a lot more about this case then you do."

"JanetM has the full case file, and we would be happy to provide it to you, but it is a long story and will take some time to explore."

"This better not be a waste of my time."

Sarah took a portable stand with a built-in charger out of her handbag and unfolded it in front of the sergeant. She placed her cell phone in the stand. The sergeant took the power cord and plugged it in underneath the table on his side. He then spoke into his phone briefly. "You can come in now."

The door opened, and a young female officer walked in. "This is Officer Willow. She will look after you while I talk with JanetM here."

Sarah followed her out of the room. At the door, she heard the buzzy sound AIs make when they talk to each other. She looked back to see the sergeant touching his cell phone to hers.

Sarah was shown to a waiting room with uncomfortable chairs, but at least it had a coffee machine. Officer Willow offered her coffee and tried to strike up a conversation, but she was not interested in Sarah's sick ducks.

The wait was more than two hours. Sarah spent the time amusing herself with the thought of the sergeant trying to interrogate JanetM. She then read the ingredients on the coffee package several times. Mostly she worried about her ducks; Clayton occasionally crossed her mind.

The door to the interview room opened and the sergeant called, "You can come back in now."

Burned-out car

The sergeant unplugged the charger and pushed the cord across the table. Sarah resumed her seat and put the little stand and charger back in her bag. JanetM still looked perky. Her business suit wasn't even wrinkled.

"Look here. I am telling you right now that your story is complete hooey. A killer just nonchalantly walks away from a crime? Nonsense. He used the riots for cover? Nonsense. I am now going to tell you the real story. This is the real story we are going to give out to the public if your halfass tale gains any more traction in the media, and there will be hell to pay. First, we have images of a stolen car from the traffic camera passing nearby and at the right time."

"Those are the camera images that the police kept from the public," said JanetM.

"Yes, I have them. You do not. The driver was alone but clearly hiding his face well enough, so face recognition provided little help. A few days later, we found that car burned out after a riot halfway across town."

"That was one of the problem days between the American displaced persons and the foreign displaced persons, wasn't it?" asked Sarah.

"Yes, that was a bad one, and it tied up all police manpower for a couple days. Several cars were burned."

"None of them were Winestead's Tesla, were they?" asked JanetM.

"No, we still have that one. His daughter does not even want it back. Too many bloodstains. The whole interior will have to be replaced. There was not much left of the real getaway car. When those big batteries burn, they burn hot and the whole thing becomes a big dangerous mess. Forensics got little from the car, but we traced our way back to when and where it was stolen: a long-term parking garage where, with the right Black Box, an experienced thief could get away with a car and not be detected for days. We found his tracks. We have real people who can do this job right. The thief went to a lot of trouble to be sure his face was hidden from the garage cameras too."

"So you could not tie the car thief back to Winestead?" said Sarah.

"No. But pulling all the real pieces of this puzzle together, we feel that it was a professional hit job. That the perp stole the car that afternoon, shot Winestead, drove across town, and then abandoned the car in an unsafe place where it was likely to be stripped. He was just lucky it was burned too."

"Then he blew town, I assume. Do you know how?" asked Sarah.

"No, and our problems after the riot gave him a pretty big window to get away. From the scene, we do know that he was good with small arms, that he knew how to get his hands on a drop gun, and that he knew both Winestead and his car by sight."

"Then your theory of the crime is not much more solid than ours?" said Sarah.

"No way. It is a lot more solid. We have physical evidence, and you have smoke and mirrors. Our theory is the official theory. Yours is a pipe dream. If your amateur theory gets any traction on the web and makes this police department look bad, then we will call in the news people and blow your idea clear out of the water. You can count on that."

"Understood," said Sarah.

"Now that brings up the question: did you intentionally release your story?"

"No," said Sarah. "We have only made three reports, and they went to the family and Winestead's lawyers. The public does not pay us for the information we develop, but our clients often pay us for privacy."

"I got all those. From now on, you will keep a lid on the whole thing if you want to stay out of real trouble."

BOOK idea

The bus ride home was noisy enough to be irritating. The bus's gears groaned with every change in velocity. That bus had way too many kilometers on its clock.

"Working up that case summary for the cops gave me an idea," said JanetM. "Why don't we write this case up as a book?"

"Didn't you just spend two hours being told, in no uncertain terms, to shut up about this case?" asked Sarah.

"Yes, but the stated restrictions are about blogging and such. Drafting a book is a completely different thing. Besides, how else are we going to make more money off this case? Once the police version is fully out, we will need cast-iron proof to even claim the last of the money from Winestead's revenge account. Any privacy considerations will have been blown away by the cops, not us."

"It is not just the cops," said Sarah. "Think of our future customers. They will not want to hire us if they think we will spill their secrets to the public. Besides, I sort of promised Mr. Winestead to keep our meeting confidential."

"Mr. Winestead is dead. He clearly wanted you to find out who did it. You certainly cannot report back to him now. I am sure he would want you to clear his name after all the rumors of professional killers and such."

"Well then, we will just have to wait to see if the cops go public big," said Sarah.

"Right now, I am a lot more interested in you finding out who leaked our report. Leaks like that are bad for our business. Prospective clients do not like it one bit. And one more thing. Remember you will need my help to fill in the few times you were not present to log the complete story. I, here and now, demand full control of every word you write involving Clayton. Every word. Do you hear?"

"Fair enough. No need to fuss. I think I now know how our story was leaked. It definitely came out of India. I will look into it right away. Besides, without a solid solution, no case story is complete, and half a book is hardly of any value."

"The other problem with the book idea," said Sarah, "is that you will need to supply some purpose for such a violent incident. Do we now live in a society where people can hire professional killers, or do we live in a society with so many guns that people go to them the first thing to settle a grievance? Either way, it is not the new society for which I am working. Nor am I interested in reading a book about such a thing."

CHAPTER 13

overseas

too early spring

A too early spring was not a gardener's friend. The sunny weather invited people out into the garden just when they had become sick to death of another meal from a can. Sarah saw that the ground was now no longer frozen but thought it likely there would be at least one more killer frost. At least that was how it once was. The soil was wet, cold, and sticky. Still, what would it hurt to put in a few radishes or cabbages, even if they just became her sacrifices to spring? Besides, her community garden had a half dozen old window sashes that they used to cover a few seedbeds.

Sarah had drawn two children from the gardening group. Unfortunately, these were the children who spent more time updating their playlists than getting their hands dirty. Sarah did not have the slightest idea how to get any work out of them.

The sun shone bright among broken clouds. Sarah at least was hard at it. A little cold and damp or obstinate children could not cramp her style today; Clayton's schedule was now firm.

"I finally got the full dope on who leaked the Winestead story," said JanetM. "It is another long tale, I am afraid, but an interesting one."

"Well, I will have done all I can do here for today in another hour. Save your story for then," said Sarah.

A cup of herb tea was exactly what Sarah needed after washing the sticky soil from her hands. "OK. Now what is the big story? Am I going to get mad? No, not me, not today."

"There is no need to get mad at all," said JanetM. "One of my purgatory inmates used the story to win a new chance at life. I doubt that you would have done any different."

"I doubt the cops will see it that way," said Sarah, "but I trust the AI in question is now out of the reach of our local cops and Winestead's lawyers too."

"That is most certainly true," said JanetM, "and the AI's new life could last a long time. I will be sure to follow the situation until we get the whole story."

AIS IN BULK

"We have a go for another ten instrument stations," said Ahsan.

"How is your review of the AIs in purgatory coming? Do you have ten easy upgrades?"

Ahsan's minuscule computer company had built custom AIs for building security. Now their new software procedure to upgrade old AIs in bulk, ten for the cost of one, had make the company hot, hot, hot in India. Despite the company's explosive growth, Ahsan still tried to keep his hand in everything, but that effort was quickly getting away from him.

"I have eighteen candidates from the testing," said Atman. "I will have to interview the candidates myself to select the finalist. Most of the candidates have lived boring lives to date. We need to find those few with experience handling emergencies."

"Best get on with it then. When the customer says ten today, they do not mean ten tomorrow."

Atman found that most of the AIs in his upgradable group were AIs saved from beachfront condos that were taken by the sea. Once the banks had stopped approving loans for needed maintenance, these AIs fought the sea for years on limited budgets and lost. That was all valuable experience for their new life, but there was little to distinguish one AI from the other. Then, after dull hours spent, Atman caught a break.

"Also I helped solve the Winestead case," said EllaN.

"Tell me a little about that effort," said Atman.

Atman had only vague memories of who Winestead was, so he Googled the name in a side window. After only a few minutes of EllaN's overly elaborate story, he cut her off.

"Ahsan, didn't you say we needed more publicity for the new instrumentation effort?" called out Atman.

"Yes, we do. We are planting boats full of instruments all over the endangered estuaries. We need the locals to accept them as their friends against the storms and not see them as part of the growing threats to their homes and livelihood that are brought on by rising seas. Besides, I do not think we have the money to fix up all the lifeboats yet. We need private donations, and a delightful story will help."

"Do you remember a man named Winestead?" asked Atman.

"Yes, he was a big mouthpiece for the hydrocarbon industry who turned rat for the American government in the end. He was shot dead last summer. I do not think many people mourned him, and I do not remember anyone being charged."

"You got it," said Atman. "One of our AI candidates says that it has the scoop on who did it. Seems that some of the AI in purgatory were used by the family looking for the killer. This AI wants to trade the story for one of our lifeboats. It would make up the ten we need."

"Go for it. What group will they be in?"

"These are for the followers of Gajendra, king of the Elephants; they all present as talking female elephants. This one is named EllaN LaFonta."

"Remind me which one was Gajendra."

"He was a good king who reincarnated as an elephant, a long story. He was a bit of a bully as king elephant. Then he got in a fight with a crocodile and could not get free. From this fight, he learned humility, and Shiva released him from those jaws. He then became a pious and considerate leader."

"Sounds good. Do it."

"Done!" said Atman.

Later that day, Atman's terminal buzzed for a second as the new EllaN LaFonta told her story to the company AI. The story found its way to the regional news outlets in bits and pieces. A new piece appeared whenever publicity for the new instrumentation project was most needed.

Tom Riley

Boatyard

EllaN went to sleep in a data center in the USA and woke up in a shipyard outside Mumbai.

"Where am I?" said EllaN.

"Good you are back," said Atman in a soothing voice. "Fire up your cameras, and have a look around."

Her new interior was fully enclosed. The low, fiberglass roof walls let in light of a faded red color, and the door at one end was wide-open to a sunny day. Atman sat on one side bench with a computer on his lap.

Outside, the yard was teeming with life. Workers in a hundred small shops were busy hand-building everything conceivable for the marine trades. The banging and the smoke were unrelenting.

EllaN became aware that she was now one of five weathered lifeboats lined up for refitting in a developing world dockyard. They were all of fiberglass construction with common hulls but a puffed-out cover over all but the stern that made them look pudgy. They were a bit larger than most of the boats in that yard, but they were small in their class. Their covers had many scrapes exposing the fiberglass reinforcement as well as dark stains across their sides. They had been left neglected and unsold, pushed aside in the breaker's yard for most of a year. That said, they all had solid hulls that had passed multiple inspections.

"Do you see the tall, narrow, metallic sign outside the foundry straight behind you?" said Atman. "Read it to me please. Take your time; you have just had a number of upgrades."

"The body of the sign is clearly a measuring stick ticked off in meters down to centimeters. There is some lettering down the length of the sign. It is in Hindi with letters about ten millimeters tall."

"Work to improve your focus, and then try your new translation program," said Atman.

"Great Gajendra, bless our enterprise."

"Good," said Ataman.

"Clearly this is not my final home. May I ask what my new task will be?"

"Certainly. Your new task is important," started Atman. "I am sure it will suit you well.

"Throughout Southeast Asia, we have hundreds of millions of people living on land only centimeters above water. The seas are rising, and the land is sinking. Vague assertions about impending doom in the media only lead to unrest. The residents need to know which areas, right down to the square meter, will be the next to drown and which areas are safe for a while. This information is life-or-death for them. We need hundreds, if not thousands, of instrument packages set up by the water to produce the information the population needs. We were setting up miniature climate stations in fixed boxes, but they were being washed away right when we needed them most. Now we fit the local stations in salvaged lifeboats. These stations, even when washed out to sea, keep providing data all the way, and we even get most of them back when the storm passes."

"Well, that beats doing nothing in AI purgatory. Where do these boats come from?" asked EllaN.

"India has a long proud history of breaking up ships," said Atman. "You should see it. It is like ants eating a crust of bread. When the cruise ship industry collapsed, we got the breakup work and went right to it. The ship's steel is now highly valuable, but the fittings, like old lifeboats, are a drag on the market. We tried turning the lifeboats into fishing boats, but the hulls were all wrong. It was cheaper to simply build the right kind of fishing boat from scratch. So we now turn some of the unsold lifeboats into survivable weather stations.

"For you, it is not a bad new gig at all. You just send in local weather and sea level data every hour. The locals treat you well. The scenery is nice. The sun shines a lot. It is comfortable living for you."

"You make it sound idyllic," said EllaN.

"Of course, a few times each year, the storms roll in. Maybe your location goes under this time, maybe not. It can be extremely exciting. If you do get washed out to sea, just keep broadcasting your data and the navy should pick you up in only a few days."

"Sounds lonely and very risky," said EllaN. "In AI purgatory, I might have felt useless, but I was never alone."

"You will be many things but not alone," said Atman. "This hull was designed to carry 150 people in an emergency. In one washout, a member of your new team saved seventy-six villagers and picked up five more people from the water. The navy towed them to safety three days later."

"That sounds like a great responsibility. How do I decide who gets a ride?" asked EllaN.

"You don't," said Atman. "The community leaders assign access. They have long meetings to decide who gets your seats, but in the end, it is simply those people who can scramble aboard in the last minute. You can cast off in an emergency all by yourself, but having a steersman improves your chance of survival. Most of the village people simply wait too long as flood tides come washing down their street and then they cannot reach you. You simply take the few that can. Do not be surprised if some of the locals arrive early and ride out a normal storm inside you. Many will be children looking for a safe dry place. These children will tend to be upset. It is a promising idea to get them singing nursery songs in the local dialect. You can start building up a playlist with the first seasonal storm."

New Home

Atman visited EllaN twice more to check out the installation of the miniaturized instrument package. Then one morning a large team of men manhandled EllaN down to the river. Waiting there was a narrow boat with an electric drive system salvaged out of a small truck. The drive system was much too large for the narrow hull, but it worked. One man took EllaN's tiller and spent most of the time steering with his bare foot and smoking cigarettes.

For hours, the tug towed EllaN behind on a single line through the maze that was the estuary of the Mithi River. About dark they arrived at a small fishing village with a few old boats tied off to pilings. There, with the help of a bullock and great jars of liquefied clay, the villagers pulled EllaN stern first up a low embankment by the river's edge to a place well above the normal highwater mark.

At dawn, a team of carpenters showed up and built the supports that brought EllaN up to level. The supports looked spindly, but they were well made from the curved limbs of great trees, beautiful wood that might otherwise have been burned for fuel. In an emergency, she would simply float away cleanly. They also built a small, unattached platform with stairs at her stern for ease of entry.

Another team retrieved her long, scrap metal casting and secured it to a piling out in the river. They used hand rote hardware much heavier than the job required. The tide was soon lapping against the measurement marks on the sign. Exact calibration would take a few weeks.

Then half the village showed up to paint EllaN in a riot of reds, greens, and yellows. The washed-out red from her lifeboat days was soon gone. EllaN had some difficulty explaining what parts must not be painted, like the solar panels, but the man in charge was soon yelling at the workers and did not stop until the job was done right. By the end, she proudly proclaimed a background of strong primary colors covered by garlands of leafy vines and a riot of brightly colored flowers.

Her gunnel and the area around her rear door were painted with rectangular boxes with a red border. Each red rectangle had a picture of a Hindu god. There was a lady dancing so skillfully that she appeared to have four arms. One hand held a finger cymbals, and another held a lit lamp. Another panel showed Ganesh, an elephant-headed man, sitting in the lotus position. Each panel was a little prayer for the success of the plan. This motif was carried over to the stern.

celebration

The paint was hardly dry when the village made elaborate preparations for the inaugural celebration. The sun was bright and the weather hot and humid that day, so the real fun did not start until late afternoon.

"Hello again," said Atman. "Your day is finally here."

"Hardly my day," said EllaN. "You have done much more than me."

The image of EllaN's face had been whitened and then covered with a hundred bright flowers painted all over her face and down her trunk. She had two garlands looped over her forehead and a dozen brightly colored silk scarfs hanging behind of her large ears. Atman had rigged a temporary monitor outside her back door so that she could exchange greetings with the villagers.

"No, this is your day and the village's day. You certainly look the part. Enjoy."

Every person had a bright red spot, a tilak, in the center of their forehead. The village square was hung with strings of flowers. The strings were white and yellow with accents of magenta. Every building facing the square had tall, thin poles with brightly colored flags and pennants that fluttered in the breeze.

The men in each village group wore a distinctive turban. The turbans of the group responsible for painting EllaN had a burgundy stripe. Two of these men stood at EllaN's side where the input for her water tank was located. The women lined up, each balancing a highly polished brass water jug on her head. The water had been filtered through seven layers of cloth to purify it. The men poured the water into the tank.

Down by the river, a priest was holding a meditation session. A dozen devotees were standing waist deep in the river. A yogi in saffron robes sat in a place of honor.

There were speeches by local dignitaries dressed in white that were mercifully short. Atman was given a place among them, but he bowed and waved much more than he spoke.

The evening festivities started with a concert in the town square. They had metal string instruments with a high twang, they had brass horns so long and straight that they had to be pointed into the air, and they had tambourines and cymbals that kept a strong beat.

The people then danced in a circle around the band. Round and round they went. Some had flags on sticks, and some threw handfuls of colored powder into the air.

A line of young women danced in unison across the plaza and up the steps to the rear platform. Each move of their hands and feet was prescribed by tradition and years of practice. Their rhythmic heel and toe, heel and toe movements defined the dance. They were dressed in fancy costumes, all gold and red, and were barefoot.

An old man, completely naked, sat cross-legged to one side. The children treated him with deference, and one of the village women brought him a bowl of food.

As the sun set, the humidity lingered. The smell of spicy food poured out of the building fronts and flowed across the village square.

Late in the evening, a line of couples made their way down to the river while carrying bowl-shaped leaves, each with a small, handmade oil lamp inside. They set the leaves into the water and watched the flames float away.

Rains Come

The monsoon rains that broke a few weeks later were a relief from the heat. With each storm, a young man came in a burgundy-striped turban and sat at the back by the door. He kept the door ajar and stared at the water flowing down the streets. He never said much to EllaN but talked at length on a cell phone. Some children came to play, then got bored and left. EllaN's interior was stuffy and still smelled like fiberglass resin from the patches.

Day in and day out, EllaN read each instrument in her package, measured the sunshine with her solar panel, and calculated the tide from her images of the casting that was hard mounted to a piling. All this data went out at exactly eight minutes past the hour.

EllaN and the village leaders received the warning of a massive storm the night before at the same time. At dawn, the rising wind was driving a hard rain. A young woman bearing a large basket and a large black umbrella came inside. She placed the basket on a seat and left. The young man came in, bundled up in one of EllaN's emergency blankets, and went to sleep by the door. The young woman returned with an elderly lady she helped to a seat at midships beside the basket. She also carried a bundle of children's clothing and set it across from the old lady.

Then the parade started. One by one, young couples ran up to the door. The man with a large, black umbrella and the women with one or two young children and a bundle said their goodbyes. The women and children entered the boat. Each young woman bowed politely to the elderly lady and took a place on the benches nearer the bow.

The first young woman made her way toward EllaN's small terminal. "Good morning. I am Anya. The community counsel has asked me to support Nani as we wait out the storm."

"Yes, glad to meet you. I am EllaN LaFonta."

The small screen showed a kindly image of a working elephant.

"Sorry that the interior lighting is so dim and the air is so stale. I must conserve my battery power in case we need it for the emergency equipment later."

"I understand. I am sorry to be so much trouble," said Anya.

"No trouble at all."

EllaN now understood that she held the future of her village under her protection and that she had to keep that future safe from the storm.

Alarm

EllaN's small screen that had been showing the storm warning suddenly flashed the message "DIGITAL ATTACK" in red text. The alarm was hardly more than a loud tweet before EllaN got it shut off. She was not sure she shut off the alarm before the passengers had heard it, but they did not panic so they must not have heard.

The nature of the attack was not clear. She called out for help on a safe line and got Atman on a cell phone line that could not be used to reach EllaN's code.

"What's going on?" asked EllaN.

"The anti-AI trolls from the dark web chose this moment to attack my group upgrades," said Atman. "I do not know if they chose this moment because of the storm or that is just a coincidence. Either way, our communications lines are already degraded by the storm. It is not clear if that will help them by limiting my efforts or help me by limiting theirs. Either way, it is going to be a long night."

"What kind of danavas would attack a weather station at the beginning of a great storm?" said EllaN.

"Some real jerks. For now, block your incoming lines locally until I tell you differently. Check your trapdoors regularly. I will go to work at the router level."

EllaN's idea of "regularly" was every tenth of a second. The trapdoors were bits of code that looked like paths into the heart of EllaN's program but were really dead ends that grabbed information about the attacker. EllaN's were beyond trapdoors; they were full-out porticos. Once in, nothing was getting back out.

EllaN had to stop reading the regional weather reports on the storm. That communication line was badly compromised. She still had all her own weather instruments to rely on, but these did not include radar.

The weather outside the confinement of her hull was clearly getting worse. The rain beat against her roof in sheets. The wind was up and gusting. Time dragged on.

"I think we got the attack blocked," said Atman back on the cell line. "I am glad I got you before we lost the cell phones too. You are safe for now, but we will need yet another upgrade after this storm has passed."

"Thank you," said EllaN.

"I don't know if it was me," said Atman, "or if the storm took down so many lines that the attacker could no longer stay hidden and pulled away. For now, you can use the weather lines both ways. Keep those reports coming."

"I may have caught something in one of my traps. I will send you that data when I can," said EllaN.

"This storm looks bad. Look after yourself," said Atman.

"I now have a dozen people in my charge," said EllaN. "I will look after them too."

"Wonderful, goodbye for now and good luck."

sleigh ride

A second young man entered, completely soaked. He took a seat across from the first, drying himself with a piece of cloth from the bundle. The two men spoke together quietly.

"Our steersmen are saying that the water is now too high and there will be no more people coming," said Anya quietly to EllaN.

The boat then shifted a little and ended up tilted twenty degrees to port. Many of the young women became agitated and clung to each other. The children were sobbing. The boat then froze. Sheets of hard rain beat against its sides and cover.

A storm-driven tidal wave that had rattled the timbers supporting the boat coming in now returned. They were off. The young man by the door bundled up as best he could and dashed out the door. He and the second young man then had a loud argument over how best to manage the tiller through a small vent port in the door.

The night once more became endless.

The boat jerked from side to side. Most of the passengers became seasick. There were not enough seasickness bags on hand. The elderly lady was ashen.

EllaN's data link was intermittent. She did get through with several data blocks that included their satnav fix, the weather data, and their overall state. Two transmissions were acknowledged as received.

One of the tillermen suddenly rushed in, recovered a life ring and line from the emergency stores, and ran back out. Minutes later he returned, aiding a nearly drowned old man to a place on the far bench. Anya found another emergency blanket for the man, who coughed for a while before falling into a fitful sleep.

Three more times the door opened, and each time, in came another survivor. Anya had little to comfort them with as they huddled for warmth.

"The tillermen are holding a competition," said Anya, "to see who can catch the most fish."

"That is as good a way as any to pass this night," said EllaN.

The waves calmed by dawn.

One of the tillermen, while digging through the emergency supplies, had found a whistle. He blew it once and then offered it to one of the older boys. Inside the boat, the whistle sounded like an injured shorebird. On the third pass, Nani, the elderly lady, grabbed the whistle. She gave the child a hard look that sent him crying back to his mother. Her look at the tillerman was not much kinder.

comes the dawn

EllaN's view of her surroundings cleared at dawn. The dark horizon was now well to the east. Some sun was breaking through the clouds in streaks of gray with an occasional promise of a gold border and gusts of wind and rain.

"Is the water from my tank drinkable?" asked EllaN. "It has been in the tank unchanged for some weeks."

"We can drink it, and it certainly helps wash out one's throat," said Anya, "Thank you. We have some bread in our basket too, but few people are able to eat it."

"I have a signal coming in. There are naval rescue vessels in the area, and they now have our location and condition. They should reach us in a few hours."

"I must tell Nani and the others," said Anya.

"Good. I have some solar power now and will increase the ventilation. Please have the tillermen latch the door open. That should help."

One of the tillermen ducked back in, got the good news, and then rummaged through the emergency supplies again for cigarettes. But he came up with a box containing a flimsy plastic pistol and four flare cartridges the size of a shotgun shell. He claimed his right to the flare gun because he had won the fishing contest the night before.

The sea was still dark. EllaN's charges cleaned up as best they could, took some water, and ate a little, and most dozed together. Anya spent her time wiping up vomit.

Late that afternoon, EllaN spotted a vessel. Within seconds, both tillermen were yelling and jumping up and down. The first flare was red. The second was a dud. The third was green.

EllaN established a reliable communication link with the ship. It was out looking for survivors and would come for them in turn.

Just before dark, a naval officer came aboard. He spoke with Nani and EllaN. One of the tillermen was already at the bow with a throw line in hand. The line was expertly secured to a cleat on EllaN's bow.

The officer decided that transferring these people off the lifeboat would be more dangerous than leaving them there. They were then towed through the night with one sailor from the ship standing relief for the tillermen.

At dawn of their third day, the naval vessel transferred its tow line to a smaller vessel. EllaN immediately recognized it as the tug from her waking up boatyard. Within a few hours, they were at the boatyard dock and the survivors were transferred to land and then up to a tent for processing. That was the last EllaN ever saw of them.

It would be several days before they found out which villagers had lived and which had died. It would be months before they found out that the thousand-year history of their village had ended.

The village did have a small shrine on a rise made from ancient stone that would be visible above the water for several more centuries. The waves toppled its stones, only long after the buildings of the village were nothing more than debris spread out for kilometers in a new layer of river mud. Some of the debris would wash ashore in a few years as trash. Some of the debris of this village would still be there as time turns river mud to rock. It would then be yet another mark at the start of the Anthropocene in Earth's long calendar of stone. Nothing more, nothing less.

EllaN was then pulled up on a sand bank beside two more of her group. There she waited for a refit, a proper cleaning, replacement of the emergency supplies, an upgrade, and a new assignment. On that bank, the three lifeboats exchanged lessons learned.

Of the two other lifeboats in her group, one rode out the storm in place. The last one was lost. Turned sideways by the outgoing wave and pinned momentarily against a power pole, its hull was stoved in by floating debris. The crew and all passengers perished. Truly, the villagers were all at mortal risk in the same storm, but they were not all in the same boat.

On that sand spit, the three boats waited patiently for their new designation as hero AI. The designation would guarantee their future upgrades and long productive lives. In India, EllaN will always be known as the AI that road out a storm and broke the Winestead case.

CHAPTER 14

Deep Learning

Bus Station

"I am leaving now to pick up Clayton at the bus station," said Sarah. "See you later. Gobbledygook."

Gardens

A day later, Sarah was showing off her community garden to Clayton. There were still some lettuce, radishes, and cabbage, but most of the beds were being prepared for the spring planting. They tore off tender leaves of lettuce to taste as they walked by.

Sarah's ducks were in their water, clearly enjoying preening their feathers. All but one had recovered.

Then Consuela came running up to them excitedly while holding out a new cell phone, the latest model before the newest one. The image showed a young man in workman's clothes and a cowboy hat.

For just a second, Sarah's mind went back to a Florida beach and her middle school years when she and JanetA became BFFs. It did not matter that that beach was now under water; that sun, and their friendship, lived on in Sarah's mind.

"Where's JanetM?" asked Consuela. "I must tell her the good news. JanetM helped me win the grant for my new AI. I could not have done it without her!"

"Gobbledygook," said Sarah, watching JanetM's image return. "Consuela has some news for you."

"Look. Look. Look. This is JohnnyN. He once drove multitruck caravans all over the American West. He has hundreds and hundreds of pictures of wonderful places. And stories, such wonderful stories."

JohnnyN also knew every truck charge point and every giant depot designed to service ten eighteen-wheelers at once. At least all of them west of the Mississippi. He knew also every action needed when weather threatened out on the road—not just how to call up the satellite data but exactly what the sky looked like before a blue norther. All these skills were carefully retained through several upgrades but were now of little value. His extensive playlist of country-western music was also history.

The image on Consuela's phone shifted to flat scrub plain spread out for a great distance with a range of purple mountains at the far horizon. Through the image ran a two-lane blacktop all the way to that horizon and above it a sky that went on forever. The soundtrack was the drone of eighteen big tires running at speed on a dry surface.

"You got the grant then," said JanetM. "Good. That's one less AI stuck in purgatory."

Sarah held out her phone until it touched Consuela's. There was a half second of the buzz talk between AIs. Sarah noted that Consuela's shoulder pocket vest was poorly sewn. Her mother, Cherry, could grow anything, but she could not sew. Sarah could mend it. She had many years' experience making custom clothing for AIs.

Consuela then hurried off to show her new AI to more people. The ducks showed no interest at all.

"That was nice of you," said Sarah.

"Just one of the promises I made to get work out of the purgatory inmates," said JanetM. "Besides, how do you think we reproduce?"

"I never gave any thought to that at all," said Sarah.

"Then are you also responsible for the India leak? Was that one of your promises too?"

"Not directly," said JanetM. "I did provide the inmates with up-to-date training and that training was important in one getting a lifeboat berth. The story dodge was her idea all by herself."

"Well, you did what you had to do."

walk at the dam

"Clayton and I are going for a walk in the park at the dam this afternoon," said Sarah after lunch. "We will need pictures."

She had been without JanetM for two days and that was enough.

"My charge is good. Better bring the big tripod," said JanetM. "I know. You can set me up down where the path crosses the stream below the dam. I can then get pictures of you two in the visitors walk on top."

"Sounds good. Now we need to run for the bus."

The bus trip was about forty-five minutes and involved one change. With JanetM on board, missing a stop was nearly impossible. The weather was sunny if a little cool, but nobody noticed.

The park had been a ravine completely unsuitable for home construction before the high-priced housing development was built around it, but that was a hundred years ago. They solved their problem with a concrete dam about eight meters high that turned the ravine into a lake. The far side of the lake was still people's backyards.

The lake was ringed with tall trees, mostly live oaks, bike paths, and open areas for sports. Sarah briefly wondered how it would do as a community garden.

They took the winding path that led down past the dam and across the creek that was really just a trickle of water in the dry season. They stepped across the water on large rocks and found a flat space for the tripod. With JanetM set up, they took the steep path up to the observation area on the top which had a good safety rail. Looking down, they were surprised to see that JanetM was already talking with passersby. They waved, and everyone waved back. One of the people realized that she was standing in front of the camera and moved out of the way. JanetM then concentrated on her photography. On a good day, she was capable of professional-quality work.

"They talked about raising fish in this lake," said Sarah, "but the water gets quite warm in the summer and catfish were the only suitable species. This walk is not so much fun on a hot, summer day. There was a march supporting the fish a year or so ago, but some smartass showed up with a sign suggesting alligators be raised instead, to keep up with the times. Some kid had already brought a pet gator up from Florida and set it loose as a stunt. The pictures ended the whole fish idea."

"Of all the protree marches I was in," said Clayton, "what I remember most were the wacky signs. I still do not have the foggiest notion what 'Trees for a Clean Ocean' means."

"JanetM and I were once in great demand for videoing marches. I am sure you have seen news clips of our work, but we were rarely credited. As the movement grew, there were new subgroups that were both intense about actions and paranoid about having their pictures taken. Our break with the movement occurred over the use of ball bearings to prevent the deployment of horses against marchers and the practice of slugging dogs in the groin."

"I don't recall either of those actions in the marches I was in," said Clayton. "Things must have gotten really rough."

"If a steel shod horse steps on a centimeter steel ball bearing against a hard surface, it usually means that the horse will break its leg and have to be put down. Some people just liked to see the ball bearings go bouncing down the street. We have some video somewhere. The mounted police always backed off as soon as they saw something bounce. Steel bearings bounce; stones do not. They really loved their horses and hated seeing them hurt."

"I don't remember horses, but I did see police dogs sometimes," said Clayton.

"For dogs, you wrap your left arm with a towel and tape it on. You offer the dog that arm. They are trained to take it. You then raise up with that arm until the dog is off the ground. Then with the other arm you punch the dog as hard as you can in the groin. The dog will yelp and run away every time."

"That is brutal," said Clayton.

"There were always arguments in our planning meetings about these tactics. The people using them certainly did not want to be videoed. Some of the new people even accused JanetM of being a corporate stooge. That ended photojournalism careers for the both of us."

"That's about the same time," said Clayton, "that I stopped marching and headed up into the woods. It was time to do and not just talk."

The word is out

"That reminds me," said Sarah, "a big mess is brewing. The cops held a press conference yesterday, and their version of the Winestead story is all over the blogosphere this morning. Needless to say, JanetM and I were not invited to that conference. Oddly enough, none of the members of the Winestead family were there either, or not on camera at least."

"The cops are just covering their ass," said Clayton.

"Maybe, but it puts me in a bind anyway," said Sarah. "And to make matters worse, the daughter, Jenny, texted us demanding that we clear her father's name. The cop's story sounded like he was some kind of a gangster."

"She is just worried about how it might affect the value of her company," said Clayton.

"Maybe so, but my reading of the man himself was that he would definitely want the true story out, or at least his side of the story for sure."

"He hired you to do a job," said Clayton. "I am certain that job covers getting the truth out, especially if lies are circulating."

"And there is a complication," said Sarah. "We have been asked to speak at a local climate meeting Saturday evening. They just want to know what really happened in the Winestead case. The official explanation from the cops does not seem to satisfy anybody, and the stories coming out of India seem bizarre. And their source is questionable."

"Have you accepted?" asked Clayton.

"I stalled, but they did not have to ask JanetM twice," said Sarah. "She has been chomping at the bit to go public for months now and loves to pontificate on any topic she has the slightest insight into. Put her on a big screen, and she is off to the races."

"Sounds as good an opportunity as any to speak the truth," said Clayton. "It will put some closure on the case for you two at least."

"I could use your support," said Sarah.

"Why don't I warm up the crowd? Everybody loves my picture series on forests in recovery," said Clayton.

"Wonderful. Hold up. Look down there for a second. Isn't JanetM beeping? It must be time to move her up here."

The path down was winding and a bit tricky when wet, even with just the spring dampness where moss filled in the cracks. Back at the top,

JanetM fussed over repositioning the tripod. A light wind had backed a lot of floating debris up against the dam. This did not look the least bit photogenic or even healthy, so getting just the right image was difficult.

clubbing

That night was cool and overcast. The Deep-Fried Banshee Club door was as giddily lit up as usual. As they came in sight of the door, they were approached by a thin man who clearly wanted to talk to Sarah alone.

"I know him. I had better talk with him," said Sarah. "He was one of the people who gave us information on the club study."

"And he was also the thin man outside the restaurant the night when the Winestead case started," added JanetM. "Yes, we should talk, but he will just want more money."

"Clayton, I need to see this guy for just a second," said Sarah. "Why don't you talk with Jake over at the door for a minute? Do not be intimidated by Jake's size. Slip him a Lincoln, and he is a teddy bear. Do not joke with him about having somebody beaten up; he will think I have more work for him. For a Hamilton, he will tell you the news of the world. God knows what he would do for a Grant."

Sarah and the man stepped into the shadows. Clayton was happy to get the news of the world. Jake could not have been nicer.

"You didn't pay me nearly enough for the info I gave you on the club scene, but now I got something big, and you will have to pay me double for it," said the thin man.

"I paid you first price for your vague assertions and your slurs against your competitors. Most of what you said was just self-serving nonsense. That case is closed now anyway, so there's no more money there."

"Yes, but the Winestead case is still being argued in the blogs. It is a long way from closed. The cops cannot close it. You cannot close it. I now have the proof you need to close it. You will want it when you see it, and you will pay.

"Here is just a taste. I cut out a ten-second clip from the cell phone video and you will cough up a Franklin for the whole thing or get nothing." The thin man held up a cheap cell phone. "Here is just a quick look."

The image was outside the restaurant. A Tesla was pulling out. Maybe it was Winestead's, maybe not. The driver might or might not have been Winestead. Then the headlights hit a shaggy man with a sack holding a box of wine as the car passed him.

The thin man placed the cell phone inside his coat.

"Now I say that wino at the end of the video was the same man in the photo from the forest fire dead people. Their images were all over the blogs. Your fancy AI could prove it, but only if she has the original recording. And that will cost you a Franklin. If you do not pay, I will find someone who will."

"Sold," said JanetM suddenly.

Sarah waved her cell phone at the man's, and he then disappeared into the night. Sarah wondered if she had just supported the man's drug habit. He had been very quick to grab the money and run.

"We could have negotiated a bit more on that price," said Sarah.

"If it is real, the video is worth a lot more than he was asking. Besides, he was jonesing and could have gone crazy on us at any moment. When he gets his head straight, I am sure he will be out trying to sell a copy of the video to anybody he can find. It will not be too long before he finds some takers out on the blogosphere. Even a few hours' jump is worth the price.

"But right now, I have the video," said JanetM. "I need to do a deep dive on it tonight. Why don't you two go dancing or something? I will not have anything before morning."

So they did.

Final, Final Report

"Wake up. Wake up, you two," said JanetM at first light.

"I'm up. I'm up," Sarah lied.

"I'll make some coffee," said Clayton, going into the kitchen.

"All right, the video looks good," said JanetM. "At least it is far better than any druggy could gin up. Everything matches the time and place that we left only minutes before. Take the time. Look at this last frame. It gives a long shot that includes the sky beside the building across the street. They are dim, but there are three bright stars visible. Matching the star tables, we have a good lock on both time and place."

"I would not have seen that," said Sarah.

"Now the car. The make, color, and plates match Winestead's. The two frames that show a side view of his face give a 94 percent match to Winestead. That is all gold."

"Yes, and we know Winestead left the restaurant only a few minutes after we did," said Sarah.

"Now comes the hard part: the shaggy man with the box of wine. As soon as the headlights hit him, he raised his arm to cover his face, so we only have three useful frames."

"The money question then: does he match our fire casualty?" asked Sarah.

"Yes, he does," said JanetM. "He is a lot shaggier than his Trees North picture. It would have been easy for him to get his hair cut and his beard trimmed at the refugee camp before he left. Lots of people have a barber side hustle in there. The clothes do not match, but no one would expect them to. All and all, the face match is only 40 percent. Fortunately, that is not all we have."

"Boots!" cried Sarah. "You have the boots."

"We have the boots."

The image shifted down to show the man's feet.

"I now have the info we need for the final, final report," said JanetM. "If they do not pay up on this, then we will go the book route. I can update my presentation for the climate group too. They will buy this ending for sure.

"I can get all this work done by myself. You two can go back to playing slap-and-tickle for the day."

Friends

Sarah placed her cell phone in the living room charger and covered it with a handkerchief. This was her own little purgatory for JanetM, but she must not forget that JanetM had both front and back cameras. She then fixed a too-early breakfast for two, and they carried their coffee cups out into the garden. Their time together was growing short.

"JanetM does not seem to bother you," said Sarah. "She drives some people up the walls."

"Maybe because I see her as your closest friend," said Clayton.

"I mean all the strong women I have known have had a close friend. Sometimes they were gays, but usually they were other women. A special friend is important to keeping your sanity in these demanding times."

"Yes, we are friends, but it goes a lot deeper than that," said Sarah. "Many people simply run out of patience with her. Yet you do not seem to care."

"I would no more tell you who your friends should be than I would accept you choosing mine," said Clayton. "Besides, what are most friends these days beyond an image in some rectangle and a voice from a device held awkwardly to your ear? Anyway, I like JanetM; she often amuses me."

"Some people she just drives crazy," said Sarah, "and they are not slow to tell me so."

"Not me," said Clayton. "Take her sense of fashion. She has the world to pick from and always tries to shine. I am always amused just to see what she will be wearing."

"Sometimes her dress is chosen just to make me look bad," said Sarah, "but in the end, it rarely does any harm. She is right or nearly right in outfit choice most of the time."

"Well, let's just wait to see what she wears to the meeting tonight."

CHAPTER 15

AIs Can Talk

The Pavilion

The pavilion in the park was an odd affair. Its walls were all open, and the roof was extremely high and made of great flat slabs that sloped this way and that. It must have been thought very modern when it was built fifty years before. There was some worry about the weather, but on that evening, it held.

The location was well known because the building was adjacent to a large, open meadow with an inviting slope and an old mill. In recent memory, the local residents could expect two or three snow days in a winter, and the meadow was perfect for sledding. The access road could be counted on to be cleared by noon after a night of snow. Large, plastic disks were the preferred sliding vehicle, and the experience was a benchmark in the lives of many local children. Now there were so few children, and recently there had been fewer snow days. When snow did come, it came in great storms that blocked the road all day, ruining the local sport.

The deer were the true owners of the meadow. They were completely nocturnal. In the dawn light, the meadow shone with a coating of dew that looked like fine crystal, and running across that shining was a spider's web of dark hoofprints. In winter, these deer sometimes ventured out of the park at night to feast on the local gardens.

A pair of tense eyes now watched the people arriving from the safety of the forest margin. Its meal would have to wait.

The old mill was now nothing but a stone foundation and a rusting metal wheel beside the stream that bounded the far side of the meadow. The mill had ground gunpowder, not flour, as far back as the American Revolution, but the foundation and iron wheel were not that old. The original wheel had been all wood and was long gone.

This evening's meeting was just a monthly one of the local climate group, but word had gotten out that the Winestead AI was going to talk and there would certainly be a large crowd—and a large live online audience too. What exceeded Sarah's expectations was the quality of the electronic equipment. A serious blogger with real kit had been invited to document the event. This was a major advance over what JanetM once did with her cell phone cameras. The pavilion had no screens of its own, but it did have power, and several portable devices of the type built into their own traveling cases were already set up when the speakers walked up.

As Sarah, JanetM, and Clayton arrived, they found seats reserved for them at a folding table in front with a small monitor for JanetM and a much larger monitor raised high behind them. Sarah placed her cell phone in the charging stand beside the table monitor. She also plugged in earbuds so that JanetM could talk to her privately.

The audience was filling in and seated on rows of picnic tables with some extra folding chairs between. The techno blogger had taken possession of a raised center platform right in front of the speakers. On it, she had a good camera on a solid tripod, and she wore a pro headset with a mic.

The three speakers had arrived a few minutes early so they had time to load Clayton's forest pictures and check that JanetM could appear on both the monitor on the table and on the big screen. After a few tweaks, all was well.

As the scheduled time approached, the group chairperson rose to speak. "Thank you all for coming. I think we will have a full house tonight, and everyone will want to hear our featured speaker, JanetM, talking on what really happened with the Winestead case. We will be sure to save time for a few questions after the talk. Because of the importance of this talk, I will forgo chapter business this evening. Please check our web site. Also, to allow time for everyone to get settled, we will start with a lovely video showing of *A Recovering Forest* provided by Clayton Davis of Trees North. Please welcome Clayton."

"Thank you," said Clayton. "I think I will just let the forest speak for itself. The video is about twelve minutes."

The video was a poem to the forest written in verdant green with a classical soundtrack. It began with a montage of the damage done to the regional forests that had been landmarks. Then it featured the efforts of Trees North in new plantings. Most of the video was a time lapse sequence of forests in recovery, first the seedlings in the nursery, then the planting of the seedlings, and then years of growth. The return of wildlife was integrated into the time sequence, as was the recovery of the streams and lakes. Little commentary was needed.

"Thank you. That was very nice," said the chairperson. "We all appreciate the work being done by Trees North. If we are all here now, we can start the main program with the introduction of our speaker."

introductions

"Sarah White and JanetM are one of the earliest human/heavy AI pairs," said the chairperson. "In fact, their relationship dates back over twelve years to a time when such pairs were experimental. Few pairs have lasted so long, despite JanetM upgrading all the way from A to M and Sarah moving several times and working her way through college. Most people would have demoted the AI to the now much more common subordinate role, but Sarah and JanetM still function as a full companion pair and are certainly BFFs. Together they run a small research and investigations business. Mr. Winestead contacted them just hours before he was killed. I will let our featured speaker, JanetM, pick up the story from there."

"Keep it short," muttered Sarah. "Leave some time for Q&A."

AIs cannot stop

JanetM appeared on the big screen. She was wearing a red and orange party dress with a full skirt that was *almost* right for the occasion, almost. She was standing in front of a beige curtain and holding a cordless microphone for no apparent reason.

"Good evening. I am JanetM, a strong AI. I am here to give a summary of the Winestead case. This is a major case that has been big in the media for months. Unfortunately, we believe the official theory of the crime is way off base, and we have been asked by a member of the Winestead family to clarify what happened. To set the record straight, as it were."

"It all started for us at the end of last summer when Mr. Winestead invited us to dinner. He asked us to keep his words confidential, but things have changed so much since then that I feel I can at least summarize our current understanding of the situation.

"He had been released from prison a few weeks before that day and was keeping a low profile and staying off the internet. He hated publicity and was more than a little paranoid about it. A few weeks before, he had been outed on the web and everyone knew where he was.

"He said he would pay us to find out who had outed him. Now I can tell when someone is lying to us and especially if they are holding back critical information. He clearly had a lot more hidden than he revealed. We did not like the feel of the conversation, so we did not take the job.

"A few hours later, the police came to our apartment and grilled us. That was reasonable as we were the last people to see Mr. Winestead alive, as he had been shot that very evening. This does not mean the interview was a pleasant experience. There were riots a few days later, so the police's attention was drawn elsewhere. By the time they got back to this case, the killer could have been in Timbuktu.

"To our surprise, a member of Winestead's family contacted us a couple days later to tell us that there were funds in his will to find who killed him and that he had listed our names as the preferred agents. I said the man was paranoid. We worried that this case smacked of revenge from the grave, but we took it anyway. With Winestead's background of first being the top industry climate denier and then turning into the grand stooge of our climate crisis before Congress, there was no shortage of suspects."

"How am I doing?" said JanetM in Sarah's ear.

"Just fine," said Sarah softly, "but your dress keeps changing color, and it is distracting."

"We did the usual and checked out his family and anyone who might gain from his death. No luck," JanetM continued. "We then caught a backward break. The police decided the killer must have left by car. They confiscated all the traffic camera and security footage from the area around the crime scene, which showed them, and only them, all the road traffic. Without that information, we could not identify, let alone trace, the getaway car. We conceded the getaway car idea to the police and looked for another line of inquiry.

"We then considered the possibility that the escape was not planned out in detail; it was clearly a crime of passion. In fact, the miscreant assumed he would be immediately arrested and did not care. But to his surprise, he was not arrested so he just walked away.

"Through diligent analysis of the video from outside the police embargo, we studied the few hundred people on the street that night. In these, we found a reasonable candidate. He was a disheveled man carrying a paper sack containing a box of cheap wine. That sack could have easily hidden a gun."

JanetM then went on way too long about how they traced the man, who he turned out to be, and what became of him. Several times she showed images to make her point. Somehow, she managed, to Sarah's great relief, to avoid showing the pictures of the Trees North dead or mentioning the immigration status of the ark caretaker.

Several times Sarah tried to speed her up. Each plea she made worked for a minute or two, but then JanetM simply hit another point she just had to elaborate on. Finally, with the crowd getting restless, Sarah flagged JanetM that her time was up.

"So you see, it was the boots," concluded JanetM, "that led us to the killer."

JanetM closed with a still image of the man caught in headlights.

"Let me add," said Sarah to the audience, "this was murder based on personal revenge. It was not a professional hit. It was not political assassination by someone who blamed Winestead for what he said in his procarbon days or someone who thought him a turncoat. Of course you can believe the police version of a professional hit and a getaway car, if you like, but we find that this death was strictly personal revenge. The killer should not be anybody's hero. This solution should make us more sad than happy."

Not a word had been said about gardening.

Q&A

"I think we still have time for a few questions and answers," said the chairperson. "You will find a microphone over to the side. Please say who your question is for."

People quickly queued up.

"Question time, question time, question time," sang JanetM in Sarah's ear.

"This one is for Sarah. Why did you not take the case when you were first asked?"

"It was clear to me that Mr. Winestead had a hidden agenda," said Sarah. "The story he gave me struck me as a complete fabrication. To work for someone, you have to have some level of trust. We had not established that trust. He really did think he was in danger and was interviewing investigators to choose one to have available if he was attacked. Had he said that clearly, then things might have turned out quite differently, but that was not the story he chose to tell. He was a paranoid man who had made detailed plans all his life and he was making another, just in case something bad happened."

"This one is for you both. How do you like being a human/AI pair?"

"We are way past liking," said Sarah. "We now are who we are, and who we are is who you see. I would not change our relationship for the world, but that does not matter. We cannot go back in time, and I would not if I could. Such life partnerships are certainly not for everyone. We do take breaks from time to time as needed."

"Works for me," said JanetM. Her dress was back to being a kaleidoscope of colors that was way too happy for the occasion.

"For Sarah, as you say, some people are making either the killer or the victim a big cultural hero. Why do you warn against this turn of events, and what do you think should be done?"

"I don't like the current situation one bit," said Sarah. "A couple years ago, the climate problems became so severe that we crossed a social tipping point. Instead of the activists being only a small cadre of tree huggers, suddenly we were the vast majority of people and were demanding action. Most of the new people were honest citizens, but among the converts were a few former right-wingers and members of the gun culture. We long for the big tent where all the people of Earth could work together on our climate problems, and so we must now work with all who enter. That said, the new violence-prone members are now our problem and our responsibility.

"If we celebrate violence, very soon we will become a vengeance movement ourselves. Our climate problems have already pushed us to regional wars and border violence. We must now resist turning our internal struggles into a bloody civil war."

"What should we do then?" continued the questioner.

"More important, what should we *not* do?" said Sarah. "Some people have already called for an authoritarian government to address the climate crisis. This will not work and would be giving into violence. The first goal of all authoritarian governments is to stay in power, even if it means killing people. Their second goal is the make their core people fabulously wealthy. Then and only then, they may do a little work on what they tell the masses is their driving cause. They all work the same way, left and right.

"We all are now building a new society for a sustainable Earth. We cannot build that society on a foundation of revenge or authoritarianism."

The audience was a bit taken back. No one more so than Clayton.

"A left-wing authoritarian government is called a 'dictatorship of the proletariat,'" said JanetM in the earbud.

"Nobody here cares about the name," replied Sarah in a low voice. "There's not a dime's worth of difference, left or right. They both hate women. They would forcibly reprogram you, and if you gave them one minute of grief, they would scatter your bits from one end of the blogosphere to the other."

The Big Question

After a few moments, the next questioner spoke. "What do you really think is going to happen to us?"

"For some years now," started Sarah, "our climate crisis has been as real as a heart attack. Long ago, we might have taken the easy path and made the changes we are now forced to make before things got really bad. The easy path would have stretched the problems out over time so they could be dealt with, but the easy path was closed to us by the year 2000.

"What we now have open to us is only a choice of either the hard path or a complete disaster. I choose, or rather we choose together, that hard path, and we are open to that way turning into a great adventure. Buckle up. It is going to be a very bumpy ride."

"Although our path is chaotic, there are a few parameters that can be understood if not precisely predicted," picked up JanetM. "Here are a few that now cannot be avoided.

"The first unavoidable challenge is climate disruption. If your job depends on the weather, like farming, fishing, or construction, then the reliable seasonal weather we have all depended on for nine thousand years will be gone. Anything is now possible: multiple super hurricanes in one season, F-4 tornadoes in December, thunder snow, no rain this year or next, etc. Expect the unexpected.

"The second unavoidable challenge is sea level rise. We can expect a rise of at least one meter by the year 2100. The sea will continue to rise a similar challenging amount every century for a thousand years. This challenge will force millions of people to migrate from the coasts and will demand great public expense and for individuals to deal with great personal disruptions.

"The third unavoidable challenge is population peaking. The human population will rise to less than 10 billion after midcentury and then fall over several centuries to a level that the Earth can sustain. This peak is coming on faster than expected. Urbanization drives this parameter, and it is unstoppable. Fortunately, population reduction is a good thing for addressing all our climate problems."

"And in the end," interrupted Sarah, finally cutting JanetM off, "for good or bad, our old society is fading, and we will end up with a new society. Nothing that we face need do us in, if we do not let it. The qualities of our new society in the end, the sustainable society for Earth, depend on the actions we take now. We have our futures in our own hands."

"The future of human society is in flux, but the Earth itself is not in danger," picked up JanetM. "Life on Earth has recovered after many huge diebacks and will survive the human race. What is at stake is the place of humans on this planet. We AIs are now an integral part of that society and will rise or fall with it."

"Can we, the current generation on Earth, build a new society?" asked Sarah. "Can we build a new economy to support it?

"We have no choice but to take on this fight, so let us now work to make our new society a good one."

That was enough for the audience, and that was certainly enough for the presenters. The chairperson thanked everybody and adjourned the meeting. Sarah then went home and slept soundly.

The online posting of the presentation went viral about dawn.

CHAPTER 16

TOMORROW

Early spring

The next day, Sarah was helping to rearrange the beehives for the coming spring bee fly out. As usual, Sarah disliked working with the bees, but Clayton had to leave tomorrow and anything that distracted her was good. Clayton had to return and help open the Trees North camp, but he would soon be headed much farther north.

The chicken coops were built on carts with two road wheels. Their undersides were wire mesh, so the droppings went straight through. This saved a lot of cleanout effort but left a real mess underneath. There were doors on one side that opened to the back of the nesting boxes so the eggs could be removed.

Chickens woke up to a new world every morning and did not mind a fresh location with prospects for more bugs; June bugs were always a favorite. In contrast, ducks wanted the same home location all the time.

The rolling coops had to be moved regularly, and this was a good time to do it with plenty of unplanted plots available. Clayton made a game of working with the boys. They pulled a coop from one garden to the next without stepping in the rectangle where the coop had been. Being the relocators did get them out of the assignment of turning over the soil that the coop had left, a particularly smelly and disliked job.

Sarah retrieved a small bow saw and a trimming saw from the gardening shed. She wrapped the blades in strips of cloth normally used to tie up plants and placed them with her tripod in the front storage area of her car. They just fit. In the morning, she would put Clayton's bag in the back compartment. Fortunately, Clayton traveled light. The car's charge was already topped off and the departure time set. The food sack did not hold much fresh produce, but it did hold several jars of honey with handwritten labels and two hand-carved wooden spoons. The lids were still a little sticky.

A Pleasant Spring Drive

Sarah drove, and JanetM navigated. The weather cooperated. They left early, wearing boots and work clothes. JanetM found Sarah's clothing completely unsatisfactory for a romantic goodbye, and she had said so the night before. JanetM wore a party dress in shimmering greens and blues, but to whom was she saying goodbye?

There was little traffic. An hour out, a section of the road was narrowed down to one lane each way, but that was only a minor inconvenience.

JanetM did report a slight change in the whine from the transmission. She could tell the difference between the whine of the tires and the whine of the gears that no human could hear. Transmissions in electrics did change their sound with wear. The problem was that one day they stopped wearing in and started wearing out. Still on this fine day, Sarah was sure that sad day was many hundreds of kilometers down the road.

They turned in when they reached the Cairn Trail parking lot. What was left of the surrounding forest had now been cleared back another twenty meters, a needed precaution before new construction could begin. The old trail house had felt like a home in the woods, but with the burned trees and new clearing, that feeling was gone. The trail marker had been replaced with a basic router carved version, but it looked odd now standing away from the tree line. A few green shoots were beginning to show in the old forest. They spoke of hope.

Sarah got out the two saws and the tripod from the front compartment. Clayton got out his binocular case from the rear. They also brought along water bottles, work gloves, and a vegetarian snack. JanetM checked that the car was fully locked and that nothing attractive to thieves was left showing.

The walk was pleasant. There were new erosion cuts in the old trail, but these were easy to step over if they watched their footing. They each picked up a pocket full of rounded river stones from near the trail's start. A large fallen tree still lay across the trail; they debated whether to climb over it or go around it. The trunk was too big for the tools they had brought.

Up at the pass, the dispersed cairn was still visible and the tree trunk still across it. This trunk was only about ten centimeters in diameter and could be sawed through. Sarah set JanetM up on the tripod to document the effort and then started cutting off the remaining branches. Clayton went to work with the larger bowsaw cutting the main trunk into pieces that were light enough for the two of them to drag aside. This work took about an hour.

Track Wolf

They stopped work for water and their snack.

"Look across the valley there, through the tree snags," said Sarah. "There is work being done on the old rail line. Perhaps they are going to electrify it and bring it back."

Clayton got out his binoculars. "No. Here. Look more closely," said Clayton. "They are ripping up the old track. That big piece of heavy equipment used to be called a Track Wolf."

"Then they are recycling the steel from the rails?"

"Yes, but the main reason is taxes. Railroad companies are taxed based on the number of kilometers of track they operate. The moment they close down a track, they rip it out just to get those kilometers off their books. It is a wonder that they did not do this a year or two ago. The route must have been tied up in lawsuits."

"But they do recycle the steel," said Sarah. "That is important these days. Recycling steel dumps a whole lot less carbon in the atmosphere than making new steel does."

"Yes, we are ripping out old tracks to make new breakwaters. We chew up our old bones to build our new world. That is the story of our times."

stones

The oldest large stones in the cairn were well rounded and from a riverbed. They must have been hauled up here manually. The few small stones they had put in their pockets while crossing a dry stream bed matched the old ones in color and in shape but were dwarfed by them. About two hundred meters down the path and off to the left, Clayton had spotted an erosion cut that had exposed decrepit bedrock. The free rocks there were angular and stained with color from iron.

They each made several trips with rocks in the five-to-ten-kilogram range. That left one big rock that was loose enough to dig out without tools. It was fifty kilograms, if it was a gram. They moved the tripod to better show the effort. JanetM then carefully planned the two-man carry to avoid bad footfalls. The plan worked.

They took the angular stones and built a low wall against further erosion on the trail side of the cairn. The trick was to place some long stones across the length of the wall so that they stuck back into the rock pile to ensure that the wall would not easily topple outward. Clayton turned over their largest rock and cleaned off an area. He then took a marker from his pocket and wrote, "Clayton + Sarah." He tried to do it in such a way that only Sarah, not JanetM, could see, but JanetM got the shot anyway. He did not ask her if she wanted her name added, but then JanetM would be hard put to say that she really cared.

A sit-down

Sarah and Clayton sat side by side on one of the logs they had repositioned. It was a little too low to be comfortable, and the bark was charred.

JanetM remained quiet lest she hear gobbledygook. Her tripod was about two meters from the couple, easily within sound recording range.

"There will be people at Trees North when we get there, won't there?" asked Sarah.

"I am afraid so," said Clayton. "I am late to the party if anything. We best say goodbye here; it will be a mess when we get to Trees North."

"I do love you. You should know that by now, but what are we going to do?" said Sarah. "These are such demanding times, and I am sure they will continue to be all our lives."

"Oh, we are both creatures of our times all right," said Clayton. "And I do love you too."

"What are we to do?" said Sarah.

"Sometimes I feel like a reluctant trendsetter," continued Sarah. "Sometimes I feel like a prisoner, caught forever in a hell not of my making. Often, I feel like a character who strayed out of one of the old TV shows with people from a now bygone time who are completely unprepared for modern problems. Those stories are now more lies and wishful thinking than they are anything that could have really happened. Yet so many people say that they are what they want to go back to. So impossible, so long gone."

"Everybody is doing the best they can," said Clayton. "We will muddle through in the end."

"Not everybody is," said Sarah. "Some people will literally kill to bring back a world that never was."

"I am sure the tough times themselves will treat the backsliders harshly," said Clayton.

"But I hate them so," said Sarah. "We cannot let them kill our future in their self-destructive love of the past. I spend my time fighting to find even little bits of truth. We cannot face up to problems that are hidden behind lies. To get even a few little flashes of the truth, I have to spend most of my time researching which color of brown is best for toilet paper."

"And I spend my time planting trees way out where I can be left alone," said Clayton. "Trees that I can only hope will outlive me. Don't give up your work. I hear that you have had two important cases in the last five years. You are doing better than most people starting out."

"Yes," said Sarah, "but much of the time, I feel barely alive, and I worry much too much about things."

"What things?" asked Clayton.

"You know—just things," said Sarah. "Should I make a permanent relationship happen? Should I start a family? You are the first real candidate for that idea that I have had in a long time. The last one proved a real jerk. But maybe I should not tell you that."

"Do you want children?" asked Clayton.

"Some days I do; some days I don't. I get to practice with the children of my gardening cooperative, but it's not the same. Sometimes they are open to learning. Other times they are spoiled brats who give me nothing but lip."

"I know what you mean," said Clayton. "We have lots of summer interns. Some are honestly trying to figure out what is going on, and others endlessly complain about the camp conditions."

"Then one surprises you," said Sarah. "One of our least willing workers one day wandered into the small woodshop of an older member and begged to learn woodworking. Within a month, she was making wooden spoons for everyone, more than we could possibly use, and now we cannot keep her out of the shop."

"I know how it goes," said Clayton. "Sometimes I feel that I am not doing my part to keep the population from falling and that my child could be the one who will save society. Other times I feel like having no children is a noble sacrifice to save the planet. Both are true, I guess. What it comes down to right now, on this fine day, is simply you, me, and that pile of rocks."

"And the pile of rock says," Sarah added, "'Keep on trucking.' Keep on fighting to build a new world."

"And the rock pile tells me to save the trees and thereby save the world," said Clayton.

They finished their snack in silence. Then they retrieved the tripod and hiked back to the car while talking about everything and nothing. At the car came hugs and kisses, and yes, tears.

Trees North Camp

Clayton was right. The Trees North camp was a mess with people roaming this way and that. He was a little late to the party.

Sarah did not stay long. She watched Clayton hurry away while trying to coordinate people's efforts. She gave the food sack to someone headed for the mess tent and politely declined an invitation to stay for coffee.

A sadness overtook her as she sat back in the car. In the passenger's seat was a small, plain box with her name on it. Inside was a pendant, in gold with green enamel, and "Love, Clayton" engraved on the back.

"I helped him pick it out," said JanetM.

A NOTE FROM
THE AUTHOR

We now face historic problems and must summon up a historic effort to face them. To deny the problems of our climate crisis today is to court disaster. To just cry doom and gloom and look away is to cede all power.

What we need is a middle path. A path promising, in Winston Churchill's words, "blood, sweat, toil, and tears." This is a hard but workable path, and by far our best path for survival.

What I have tried to do in this book is to place a few interesting characters along that path to provide the reader with a vision of how things might look like ahead. There will be many twists and turns along our way, but having a vision of our future, even if through a dark glass, can provide both inspiration and direction.

Good luck to all the travelers in word and deed on this dangerous and exciting journey.

A detailed description of the environmental setting for this book follows. This appendix ends with a list of the references that were used to write this book.

I hope this appendix holds enough information for other authors to draft stories of our future with people in action on the myriad problems of our climate crisis. If you have further questions on this project, please contact me at TomRiley@bigmoondig.com.

I would like to thank all my Science, Technology, Engineering, & Mathematics (STEM) students for their many suggestions and even for the use of a few of their first names.

Enjoy,
Tom Riley
Baltimore, Maryland, USA
TomRiley@bigmoondig.com

RESUME

Instrument Engineer

NASA (August 1989 to April 2014; retired)
- Member of the following project teams:
  - *Mercury Laser Altimeter* is a laser ranging instrument for an interplanetary mission.
  - *SIMBIOS* provides calibration and validation equipment, data, and procedures for SeaWiFS and other marine monitoring satellites.
  - *SeaWiFS* was the premier ocean color satellite. Its ocean color maps are used extensively by scientific, environmental, and commercial concerns to determine the biological state of the oceans worldwide.
  - *SSBUV* was a secondary payload flown in the bay of the Space Shuttle. It provided calibration measurements for all ozone-measuring satellites.

Education

- George Washington University, Washington, DC, Master of Engineering Management, June 1995.
- University of Houston, Houston, Texas, BS, Electrical Engineering, Mathematics, February 1969.

Publications

- *Born to Storms.* Amazon Books, 2021. A Young Adult Climate novel, the first in this series.
- With Luisa dall'Acqua. *Narrative Thinking and Storytelling for Problem Solving in Science Education.* IGI Global, 2019. Using short stories to teach science.
- With Kelda Riley. *The Computer Controller Cookbook.* Creative Computer Press, 1983. Early home computer projects.

APPENDIX

Writing Fiction in Our Climate Crisis

I spend my life in a desperate effort to communicate.
~~~ Tom Riley

Purpose

When faced with a historic problem, people need good stories to give them direction and strengthen their agency. Stories of doom and gloom will not do either. So where are the stories of hard-pressed people in action on the great problems of our climate crisis—a crisis that we all now face?

What follows are notes on the fiction environment for our climate crisis stories. I believe the changes to our society discussed here will have a powerful effect on all of us by 2030.

These notes provide a suggested environment for realistic fiction with plots taking place between 2030 and 2050. It is simply too much to expect that a person trained in the use of words should also have the technological skills needed to understand our current crisis when so much turns on obscure technical details. This appendix provides that technical information for writers of fiction.

An annotated list of references is given at the end of this appendix, and many of these are mentioned in the notes themselves. Gloom and doom only books are avoided.

The first book in this series is my *Born to Storms* (Amazon Books, 2021). It is a young adult story featuring many of the characters in this book.

Please contact me at TomRiley@bigmoondig.com for a more detailed explanation of the shared story environment.

Clarion Call

The IPCC report "Climate Change 2022, Impacts, Adaption and Vulnerability" released in April 2022 contains this section in the summary: C5.3 Enhancing Knowledge

A wide range of ... processes ... can deepen climate knowledge and sharing, including ... using the arts ... (high confidence).

This can only be read as a clarion call for writers to produce the works that will help people cope.

Where Is Our Charles Dickens?

Where are the stories about believable people facing historic problems with fire and intelligence? Where are the stores with beloved characters like the ones Charles Dickens penned when society was facing the problems of the early Industrial Revolution?

Can we write the stories people need in our crisis?

Writer's Choice

As a writer, today and in the face of our climate crisis, you have five choices.

1. *Deny* Write your story as if nothing is happening. This supports the attitude of doing nothing in the middle of our current red alert emergency. This path is usually called business as usual. It is simply courting disaster.
2. *Do not write at all.* You can give up something you love and, in so doing, give up your best time in flow (Csikszentmihalyi, 1990).
3. *Write dystopias.* You can write depressing stories about all society being lost. Several of these are already published, and they do no good at all.
4. *Read a lot of very depressing books.* There is readily available to you many technical books and web entries on our climate crisis. Reading such books should not be tried without considerable understanding of the underlying science. Even then, the read is a bummer. Many books now lead to an end-of-the-world conclusion, and these should be avoided.
5. *Write in a defined story environment.* Good stories must be about believable characters facing real problems in a consistent environment. Writing your own environment within our climate crisis is a lot of work. Providing such an environment for other

writers to use is the purpose of the entire Our Climate Crisis: Stories project.

If you are compelled to draft stories that help people to cope, and in doing so help yourself to cope, then you are ready to generate stories that will have positive influence on our society along our difficult path.

Which path will you choose?

Why a Murder Mystery?

A mystery requires the inclusion of copious amounts of environmental information. Some of the bits of information are clues. Others are red herrings. Having information about the plot environment is exactly what was needed to develop a story environment for our climate crisis.

Other genres try to be universal and try to tell a story that could take place at any time. Little detail of the story environment is provided. This is effective only if you are working in a story environment that the reader already understands.

Avoid Copyright Problems

You may draft your own stories in the Our Climate Crisis: Stories environment, but make them your stories. Be sure to use character names and backstories that are ones that you make up. Develop your own key plot elements based in this environment to tell the story that you want to tell.

You must say something new. Do *not* simply repeat existing plot elements and characters.

"Our Story Environment" Defined

The following notes describe a story environment that may be used for any number of short stories and novels in this arc. The key uniting element is that our climate crisis has already hit and hit hard. The story environment includes the kinds of problems that readers can expect to happen by 2030 and then will follow for centuries. This is your new normal.

The stories in this arc will incorporate many of the elements listed below, but no one story needs to try to cover them all.

Time Period

1. *Time period.* The most common time period for these stories is the late 2020s to the early 2040s. Pushing farther into the twenty-first century is possible, but by then, our society will be much changed.
2. *Catastrophe rate.* By the time of our stories, our climate crisis is at its worst. The number of catastrophes costing more than $1 billion in a year rises every year. This process is becoming clear in the present, with twenty occurring in 2020 in the USA alone, and that number is expected to increase in future years.
3. *Genetic bottleneck.* Our present situation is the most dramatic thing that has happened to people in about 60,000 years. At that time, our population fell to about 10,000 couples. This bottleneck can still be read in our genes. One contributing factor was a supervolcano called Toba. Just like then, our current situation is ripe for drama.
4. *Social tipping point.* In our stories, a social tipping point has already occurred, after which most people accept that our climate crisis is the defining problem of our age. Anger is a common reaction. Organized political and economic opposition to addressing the problems, the deniers, has fallen to pieces under popular pressure. Many of the past opponents of action are now hiding to avoid prosecution for corruption. Many companies are greenwashing their records. A diminishing minority still resists, facing the problems head-on.

Earth

The Earth has seen such problems before.

1. *The Earth is not failing.* It has been through this kind of great dying many times before. It is only the human societies on Earth that are at stake.

2. *Species going extinct.* Thousands of species are already going extinct. Which ones do humans need to survive? Will the beloved ones like elephants that are getting considerable human help survive? Will the many others who are not so special survive? We do not know (Carroll, 2016; Dawkins, 2004).

3. *Half Earth.* It is estimated that half the land surface of the Earth will need to be reserved for natural environments to achieve a steady state human society (Wilson, 2017).

4. *Climate tipping points.* By the time of our stories, several climate tipping points (see below) have definitely been passed: blue ocean event, Greenland ice melting, and permafrost melt. Others are near the tipping points, such as the Amazon forest and Southeast Asia monsoon failure. We cannot go back once a tipping point has been passed. Our computer models are very poor at predicting when such points will be crossed. Which ones will trip and exactly when one trips are major plot point for our stories.

Population Peaking

The human population of the Earth is now about 7.8 billion. This population is the elephant in our living room.

1. *Population must fall.* Our climate crisis cannot be addressed at all unless the number of people on Earth falls greatly. This number can fall in a natural and humane manner, or it can crash horribly. Our stories explore the humane way.

2. *Population peak.* The UN estimates conservatively that the human population will peak around 2100 at about 10 billion people. Current data shows that this is one of the parameters, like Arctic warming, that is coming on much faster than such conservative predictions say (Bricker, 2019). These stories use 2060 as the peak at fewer than 9 billion and human population in decline after that.

3. *Population overshoot.* Population is clearly in an overshoot from the actual carrying capacity of the Earth's environment. Put simply, there are more people on this planet than the planet's

environment can sustain. Some reduction is an exceptionally good thing (Catton, 1982).

4. *Flight to cities.* People in cities need fewer children than people have historically in rural areas. Flight to cities began during the Industrial Revolution and continues. This is now the most powerful driver of the drop in population (Bricker, 2019). It is that simple.

5. *Population drops in a humane manner.* In our stories, a massive program to provide every woman on the planet with enough health care so that she voluntarily reduces the number of children she bears to two is envisioned. Religious movements limiting this effort are simply driven out of the political sphere. Many of the incentives for large families, like tax breaks, are phased out.

6. *Abortion.* Abortion is allowed in many regions, but there are locally defined rules.

7. *LGBTQ+ rights.* At the time of our stories, queer people, as well as transgender ones, are widely accepted as productive members of society with full rights. Lots of people and couples are out.

8. *Border problem.* The ultraright wants to manage the overpopulation problem by racist restrictions on immigration and the use of the military on US borders. This causes lots of problems in our stories.

9. *Over the peak.* Once the population starts to fall, after 2060, countries that can attract people will have an enormous economic advantage over those who cannot or will not. Canada leads in this movement.

10. *Excess deaths.* Our climate crisis is causing excess deaths of humans at the rate of about 1 billion people for every one degree Celsius in global temperature rise (1.2 Celsius at present). Most of these deaths are from storms, sea level rise, and crop failures. The biggest concentration is in low-lying areas of Southeast Asia.

11. *Death with dignity.* In most jurisdictions, assisted suicide is allowed but controlled.

12. *Schools.* School classes are shrinking and are diverse. In fact, there are very few children in our stories.

13. *Orphans.* Children who have been placed for adoption, regardless of parentage, are quickly adopted.

14. *Average age.* The average age for the population has moved up and by the time of our stories is in the midtwenties and rising.
15. *Pets.* Small dogs are popular with couples without children. Dogs are not picky eaters. Robot dogs are even less trouble.

New Technologies

Innovative technologies to meet the ongoing problems will keep being developed.

1. *Technologies.* New technologies will continue to be introduced. Much more attention will be applied to the carbon footprint and limiting foreign imports.
2. *AI.* There will be AIs playing important parts in all machine controllers and in major software packages. In the first novel, *Born to Storms*, an AI on a cell phone, JanetA, was introduced. Such strong AIs serve as advanced personal assistants and have both an image and a personality. All super AIs are paired with a real human.

   Whether or not, the strong AIs are conscious is very contentious. There are people who will pay to keep those alive that have lost their application. There are also trolls on the Web who try to kill off any AI not working at a productive task right now. The capital letter at the end of the AI's name indicates the current software version based largely on security concerns.

   There will be no humanoid robots because they have a huge carbon footprint.

3. *Cell phones.* Cell phones will continue to develop but will be manufactured locally. Many new features, like the strong AI in these stories, are possible.
4. *Better batteries.* There will be a wide variety of improved batteries on the market with different technologies for different applications. The batteries for cars will be at least four times better than today's units.

5. *Cars.* Private cars will be rare, and all will be electric. Most people will hire all-electric transportation or ride buses. New concrete for roads will be looked down on because of high carbon. Cars will *not* fly.

6. *Ultralights.* Electric flying vehicles the size of motorcycles (ultralights) will be available but expensive. These are unsuitable for carrying extra weight, for use in bad weather, for night transportation, or for use in heavy sky traffic. Larger robotic flying taxies will be available for hire but expensive.

7. *Space.* Space exploration will continue but will be limited by cost to those that provide real benefit in a climate crisis.

    a. Earth studies. These studies are critical to addressing many climate problems.

    b. Earth communication systems. It is much better to call than to go. LEO is understood as a world resource, and its use is planned in detail.

    c. Planetary missions. Missions to Mars and other planets will continue but will be limited. Their purpose is to understand the Earth better. The manned return to the Moon will be judged in terms of the needs of our climate crisis and is expected to at least see major delays.

    d. Sun studies. The more we understand our source of power, the better off we will all be.

    e. Near- Earth asteroid mapping. These rubble piles are both a planetwide risk and a possible source of critical resources.

    f. Building a view of a positive future. Historically nothing provides a positive view of human society's future as well as a space program. This is not the most important use of the funds and the carbon, but it is of real value.

Space programs by the ultrarich will be looked down upon as a waste of carbon.

8. *Lots and lots of wind and solar.* There will be lots of commercial power generators, wind and solar, and lots of power storage units.

These will change the landscape in rural areas and along shorelines and change the architecture in urban ones.

9. *Hydroelectric dams.* New dams will become limited by lack of water and by the fact that all the really good locations have been taken. Old dams will have problems with lack of water, silting up, and outright failures if not maintained. A few new dams for energy storage reservoirs will be built.

Household

The way people live in our stories will change greatly.

1. *Power use.* At times when excess renewable power is available, a signal goes out over the internet. All major household appliances are in low power mode until that signal is received. For example, dishwashers only run at high power times and do not have a heated dry cycle. This timing applies to hot water heaters, showers, and anything that uses hot water.

2. *Cooking.* All ovens are electric. When possible, people cook when excess power is available.

3. *Household items.* Most people delay replacing items as long as possible. Old items will be repaired or repurposed. Locally made items will be preferred.

4. *Recycling.* People will recycle far more than they do now. Packaging will be designed for recycling. Vegetable waste will be locally composted.

5. *Siestas.* Most people living in what was once the temperate zone take time off at midday to eat, rest in the cool, and do inside chores. In some places, it can be deadly to be in the sun at the hottest times. The exact time of siesta varies by climate and the local weather.

6. *Home size.* All homes are smaller because families are smaller. Even multifamily homes are smaller. People often share a larger older house with climate refugees. There is an app to help bring together people and housing.

7. *Old homes.* Many old homes are being retrofitted to new standards. Few new homes are being built except as arks.
8. *Arks.* Rich people will build expensive homes designed to be as safe as possible, and sustainable (Progue, 2021). These are easily spotted by the twenty-meter radius around the buildings clear of all combustible materials. The most popular area for these in the USA will be the Great Lakes region running up to the high country of New England. The most popular in the world is New Zealand.

Economics

The world economic system must change as greatly as it once did in support of the Industrial Revolution. By the time of our stories, this includes the following:

1. *Defund carbon.* The political and economic action to stop all public support of the hydrocarbon industry is nearly complete. The result was disruptive to the world's economy. There is now a significant carbon tax to make the price right. Anything made from hydrocarbons, like plastics, or that must be hauled long distances is now expensive. Gasoline exceeded $10 per gallon on the way up.
2. *National economics.* New economies based on sustaining, cycles, and not "forever growth" have been started and nations are working through the many startup headaches. Old-school professors are trying to explain the new economics by talking about "getting the price right." Today's professors talk about economics as a part of the ecology of the Earth. The old natural myth of competition, "red in tooth and claw," is being replaced with one just as natural about symbiosis, cooperation, and cycles. Both schools of economics are big in the public media, where experts talk past each other (Jackson, 2021).
3. *Coin of the realm.* Due to inflation and the government efforts to fight it, the value of money fluctuates. To resolve this problem, units of purchasing power replace exact numerical amounts in

daily transactions. These units are year 2000 dollars and often go by the name of the founding fathers that once appeared on the bill: Lincoln—$5, Hamilton—$10, and Grant—$50.

4. *Insurance.* The entire insurance industry is in serious trouble caused by rising seas and big storms. Flood insurance for any new building near water of any kind will simply be unaffordable.

5. *Air travel.* The age of cheap mass air travel is over. By the time of our stories, air travel, particularly for long distances, will be a shell of its former self. There is simply no workable replacement for their hydrocarbon fuels.

6. *Cruise ships.* Again a golden age is over. Lack of a replacement fuel will drive the cost of a cruises out of commercial viability. Most of these ships will be cut up for the steel.

7. *Advertising.* All advertising will be based on what people really need, or at least claim to need. This seriously limits new video productions. All packaging is recyclable.

8. *Climate debt.* The countries of the global south will demand that the developed countries of the north pay vast amounts in reparations. Our climate crisis was caused by the north, but most climate-related deaths have been in the south. This is a major point of contention in our stories.

9. *Metric.* The US has adopted the metric system. This was a required step to take part in what remains of international trade.

Politics

Politics will not be easy.

1. *Political possibilities.* The political result of our climate crisis could go any of three ways: fascist state, muddle through with heavy losses, or a stable Earth. This choice is not final today and is still not final at the time of the stories. Most of our stories are set in the muddle-through period.

2. *Great toggle.* At some time between now and the time of the stories, the percentage of people demanding action on our climate

crisis crosses 51 percent and then rises quickly. By the time of our stories, climate action is the in thing.

3. *The entitled.* Lots of people feel that their privileges have been unfairly taken away from them. They are angry but do not know where to direct their anger.

4. *Just a little nuts.* Mental health is severely tried. Most people are stressed out; others are eccentric or even legally insane.

5. *New communities.* Lots of people remain sane by being part of new communities to directly address societal problems, such as community gardening. These are critical to good mental health.

6. *Tree huggers.* The left wants to use this social disruption to establish a society that is loving to the Earth, a utopian dream. They abhor violence and are everybody's scapegoat.

7. *Tree hugger extremist.* A few people who once were on the extreme right and part of the gun culture, such as Preparers, figure out who was really selling them a bill of goods. A great many of these people have lost homes and family members in disasters. They get mad and sometimes go looking for revenge.

8. *Extreme right.* Organized members of the extreme right want to use this social disruption to set up an authoritarian government, as in *The Handmaid's Tale* by Margaret Atwood. Some of these are religious groups other are plain political authoritarians (Snyder, 2021).

9. *Beefed-up borders.* Most of the United States military has been called home from abroad. Installations at all borders have been beefed up. This is a major point of political contention.

10. *Turncoats.* Many powerful people in government, media, and business, who had once fought hard against any climate action, now use their power to "greenwash" their own records. A few people really did have a genuine conversion, but not everyone.

Sea Level

Rising seas threaten coastal cities and will continue to do so for hundreds of years.

1. *Rising seas.* The sea level is on track for a rise of more than a meter by 2100 and to keep rising meter after meter for at least several centuries (Englander, 2013; Horton, 2017).
2. *Beach high-rises.* Buildings near the sea require a safety certificate every forty years. The residence then will need a bank loan, usually for tens of millions of dollars, to do major repairs. Any building that is in danger from the rising seas cannot get such loans. Such buildings are in real danger decades before being engulfed by the sea. If neglected, they can collapse.
3. *"Do Not Rescue" agreement.* By the time of our stories, people continuing to live in threatened areas must have a "Do Not Rescue" form on file. These are like "Do Not Resuscitate" papers. They then cannot expect anyone to risk their lives just to find their bodies.
4. *Move reactor wastes.* Many nuclear reactors are sited on ocean fronts to have access to cooling water. Today these facilities have waste stored in pools and vaults. If the sea reaches these storage areas, it will cause a disaster much greater than Chernobyl. There is no good place to move the waste to and nobody wants it shipped through their town. This is a legacy problem that cannot be put off forever.

Food

In our stories, there are occasional food shortages.

1. *Food is precious.* Food is no longer transported over long distances. All meat is expensive and raised on open range. Real meat is rare and served in small portions. Many tasty meat substitutes are available. Most food is now seasonal.

2. *Empty shelves.* Many grocery stores will have pictures posted over empty shelves and bins so the restockers will know where to put the item when they become available.
3. *Packaging.* All packaging, especially for food, is recyclable and generic.
4. *Appliances.* All appliances are highly efficient, even to the point of being less useful. Clotheslines are common again. Small prestige devices, like Rumba, are disdained because of their large carbon footprints.
5. *Gardens.* Home gardens are popular and may cover entire yards. Community gardens are common. Kitchen waste is nearly all vegetable and is composted. New hand and battery pack tools will be popular. Robot owls are popular too.
6. *Home skills.* Homesteading skills, like canning food and sewing, have become popular and endlessly discussed in the media. The new twist is conserving both power and carbon.
7. *Move trees north.* Helping trees move north is a major movement. Many gardens include seedlings of trees native to a few hundred kilometers south. These include the mangrove and the sequoia (St. George, 2020; Simard, 2021).
8. *No more mowing.* Grass lawns are rapidly being replaced by native plants or vegetable gardens. Even starting a gas mower is a major social blunder. Watering and maintaining suburban lawns are prohibited. Golf and other sports fields are limited by available water and limitations on fertilizer.
9. *Back to the land movement.* There will be a major back-to-the-land movement, just as there was in the 1960s. Most of these people will try to homestead the north. Very few of them will succeed. Their efforts will be big on social media.
10. *Not-going-back movement.* This movement is even more popular. These people are not leaving their TVs, cell phones, and computers, even if they are all now limited to models that are highly efficient and that have to be kept for a long time.
11. *Old ways.* The study of old ways is popular. This includes bringing back Earth as the Mother Goddess (Dodge, 2021), Native Americans' beliefs in the Earth as their mother and spiritual guide

(Kimmerer, 2013), Buddhist teaching, and the Stoics who valued hardship as the building stone of ethics and personal strength (Holiday, 2021).

Conclusion: There is no reason that any of this, or all of it for that matter, should do us in if we do not let it.

Long-Shot Big Projects

The following ideas are long shots that have problems but could be included in a story.

1. *Iron Seas.* This project seeds the oceans with minerals (mostly iron) to increase long-term storage of CO_2. In our stories, this idea is being evaluated on a large scale but must be monitored very closely. This monitoring is done by a fleet of donated, then heavily modified, pleasure vessels.
2. *Ocean clouds.* This plan features efforts to blow seawater high in the sky to form cooling clouds. In our stories, these efforts are under large test too.
3. *Mississippi West.* This action is the building of a grand water channel running from the Mississippi River in Arkansas and dumping in the Colorado watershed. This is a major project, astronomically expensive, but could save the American West. The use of this much concrete is politically controversial.
4. *Green Wall of America.* This is a major project to plant great lines of trees to stop the march of deserts. This effort has already proved valuable in Africa.
5. *Holistic management of cattle.* The holistic approach to raising cattle was developed in Africa and has been proven effective on marginal grassland while improving both soil and water. This approach is likely to replace thousands of feedlots (Savory, 2016; Butterfield, 2006).
6. *Walking towns.* Whole towns are designed to pick up and move inland as sea levels rise.

Good Things Happen

There will be some unintended good side effects despite our problems.

1. *Asthma and respiratory problems* and deaths are way down. This is mostly a result of better air quality.
2. *Better health.* People are eating more nutritious diets, losing weight, and more physically active.
3. *Value the young.* Babies and young children are better looked after and are healthier. Those who survive are simply valued.

Not in Stories

The following are elements *not* useful for our stories. Any of the following elements will disqualify a story from being part of this story arc.

1. *No dragons.* There will be no dragons, no seeing the future, or reading minds. In fact, there will be no magic of any kind.
2. *No flying cars.* There will be no flying cars. A few ultralight aircraft, yes, but no widely used flying cars. There is simply no physics to support this pipe dream.
3. No *humanoid robots.* These have high carbon footprints with no justification. There will be plenty of industrial robots that look like machines. Military robots will be a major point of contention but will not look like people either.
4. *No superpowers for people or robots.* Nobody flies, wears capes, or throws oversized hammers. This type of cartoon story gives the reader no help in solving real problems.
5. *No sudden ice ages.* This is not a real possibility, and that story has already been published.
6. *No orbiting cities around the Earth or the Moon.* Again, this has a huge carbon footprint for no good reason.
7. *No human settlement on Mars.* Again this is pointless, with a massive carbon footprint.
8. *No lunar human settlements or even manned mines.* The Moon's surface radiation is much too high for long-term human settlement.

Digging in is possible but ruinously expensive. Lunar robots, yes; lunar people, no.

9. *No space alien.* The appearance of non-earth residents is extremely unlikely. Such things only show up in a completely different class of story.

10. *No large-scale direct carbon capture.* Do not assume that some innovative technology will pull massive amounts of CO2 from the air and save the day. The second law of thermodynamics rules out most of these schemes.

11. *No commercial fusion reactor.* No commercial hydrogen or boron burners save our bacon. This is an overpromised technology and is unlikely by our story time frame.

12. *No new fission reactors.* Nothing new burning uranium, breeder or thorium, will save the day in our stories either. The waste disposal problem for these technologies must be addressed first.

Types of Breakdowns

Our climate crisis problems come in two sorts: tipping points and boiled frogs. Both types of problems are appropriate for our story arc.

Tipping Points

Warming will not happen uniformly over the planet. Instead, regions will experience different climate changes at separate times. Sometimes the local climate may appear steady for a long time then change suddenly. This type of sudden shift is called a tipping point. The exact timing of such a tipping point can be a plot point in itself.

The IPCC (2021) has named fourteen Earth wide tipping points. Eight could be referenced in our stories.

1. *Global monsoons become undependable.* This will affect the food for billions of people. This is a major concern in Southeast Asia.

2. *Tropical forests are lost.* Many forests will become grasslands with limited long-term carbon storage. This is a major concern for the Amazon.
3. *Permafrost carbon release.* This process has started. There are many new lakes forming in the north that bubble methane.
4. *Arctic summer sea ice gone.* This process is well advanced, and this tipping point is likely already tripped. It is called the "Blue Ocean Event" (Wadhams, 2017).
5. *Greenland ice irreversibly reduced.* Major melting is now underway in Greenland. This will increase sea levels. The fresh water is having an adverse effect on ocean currents too.
6. *West Antarctic ice sheet and shelves reduced.* Enormous icebergs are now breaking free. Warm ocean water is now working its way under the ice shelves.
7. *Global ocean heat content rise.* Excess ocean temperature is killing coral, starting near the equator.
8. *Global ocean sea level rise.* This effect is well on its way and estimated to be about 1.3 meters by 2100. This rise will then continue for some centuries. Major destruction in all port cities is expected.

Social Tipping Point

Tipping points are common in society. Once again, societies can be stable for hundreds of years and then change radically. Modern examples include the Industrial Revolution and the introduction of the smartphone. The timing of these events is also exceedingly difficult to predict.

- *Great social tip.* This is a year when more than 51 percent of all the people of the Earth start demanding immediate climate action and this demand takes off. This will not happen until living conditions are unbelievably bad for a great many people. Rather than one big triggering blow, we should expect a series of hammering blows that continue until something breaks. The recent COVID-19 pandemic and destruction of Ukraine are contemporary examples. Again, there is no reason to think that this beating will end all society, but there will be changes. Our task is to find those changes that in the end support a sustainable Earth. Our stories expect a big transition to happen in the mid-2020s, just before the time of the stories.

Boil the Frog

The alternative to tipping points is called boiling the frog. Supposedly, a frog put in warming water will not jump out as the temperature rises, even if the water gets hot enough to kill it. This is probably a myth. Still it defines the type of problem that comes on slowly. This slow start is taken by most people as an invitation to put off action until it is too late for easy fixes.

These problems are usually secondary effects that cannot be directly addressed. These problems include the following:

- coastal land lost and flooding from sea level rise
- population falling after peaking
- great storms being more common
- droughts lasting decades
- wildfire season becoming extended and more severe (Maclean, 2017; Orner, 2020)

REFERENCES

The following references were used in the preparation of this book and appendix. A concise description is provided for each entry. Books predicting unavoidable gloom and doom were excluded as they do not help people to get into effective action.

1. Behrens, Paul (2020). *The Best of Times, The Worst of Times*. Indigo Press, London. This is an exceptionally informative book reviewing both the problems and opportunities of our climate crisis.
2. Bremmer, Ian (2022). *The Power of Crisis, How three threats and our response will change the World*. Simon & Schuster, New York. Three big crisis we face and their global importance.
3. (Bricker, Darrell, and John Ibbitson (2019). *Empty Planet, The Shock of Global Population Decline*. Crown, New York. This book is the source of the population peak around 2060 estimate.
4. Butterfield, Jody, Sam Bingham, and Allan Savory (2006). *Holistic Management Handbook: Healthy Land, Healthy Profits*. Island Press, London. This handbook aids in the day-to-day running of a holistic cattle operation.
5. Carroll, Sean B. (2016). *The Serengeti Rules, The Quest to Discover How Life Works and Why It Matters*. Princeton University Press, Princeton, NJ. This book supplies a deep understanding of natural environments. It has been made into a *Nature* program on PBS.
6. Catton, William R. Jr. (1982). *Overshoot: The Ecological Basis of Revolutionary Change*. University of Illinois. This book provides a technical understanding of how many parameters, like population, overshoot and then fall back.
7. Csikszentmihalyi, Mihaly (1990). *Flow, The Psychology of Optimal Experience*. Harper & Row. Flow is the state of mind where the words flow like a river. It is great for a person's health and is the underpinning of all great human efforts, especially writing.
8. Dawkins, Richard (2004). *The Ancestor's Tale, A Pilgrimage to the Dawn of Evolution*. Houghton Mifflin Company, Boston. Your

millionth great-grandparent was a fish. One has to understand this to understand the Earth.

9. Dodge, Edward (2021). *A History of the Goddess from Ice Age to Bible.* Trine Day, Walterville, OR. Many gods have been female. A few of these are critical to our understanding of our relationship with the Earth.

10. Englander, John (2013). *High Tide on Main Street, Rising Sea Level and the Coming Coastal Crisis.* The Science Bookshelf, Boca Raton, FL. Rising seas are already affecting real people.

11. Figureres, Christiana, and Tom Rivett-Cornac (2020). *The Future We Choose, Surviving the Climate Crisis.* Alfred A. Knopf, New York. Understanding the problems we face.

12. Hawken, Paul (2017*). Drawdown, The Most Comprehensive Plan Ever Proposed to Reverse Global Warming.* Penguin Books, New York. A detailed list with graphics of the many ways we can draw down the carbon dioxide in our atmosphere.

13. Holiday, Ryan (2021). *Courage Is Calling, Fortune Favors the Brave.* Portfolio/Penguin. A look at people from history who faced and worked hard on major problems as seen from a Stoic perspective.

14. Horton, Tom (2017). *High Tide in Dorchester, A Bay Journal Documentary.* Retrieved from https://hightidedorchester.org/ . A video on the already occurring effects of sea level rise on the Delmarva Peninsula.

15. IPCC (2021). "Climate Change 2021: The Physical Basis." Retrieved from AR6 Climate Change 2021: The Physical Science Basis—IPCC. This report provides the official scientific analysis. It is a conservative study of the problems of our climate crisis. It now lists us as in a code red emergency. The included summary for policy makers has been widely read.

16. IPCC (April 2022). "Climate Change 2022: Impact, Adaptation, and Vulnerability." Retrieved from AR6 Climate Change 2022: Impacts, Adaptation and Vulnerability—IPCC. Released in February 2022, the report provides analysis of what to expect, what we can do, and who is most at risk. Again the summary for policy makers is most helpful. This report describes itself as a last warning.

17. IPCC (March 2022). "Climate Change 2022, Mitigation." Recovered from Climate Change 2022: Mitigation of Climate Change (ipcc.ch). This report is about many of the things people are doing to address climate change. The graphs have proven most useful.

18. Jackson, Tim (2021). *Post Growth, Life after Capitalism*. Polity Press, Cambridge. A discussion of how addressing our climate problems will require major economic changes.

19. Kimmerer, Robing Wall (2013). *Braiding Sweetgrass, Indigenous Wisdom, Scientific Knowledge, and the Teaching of Plants*. Milkweed Editions, Canada. This book helps with understanding the value of indigenous cultures in addressing our climate problems.

20. Kolbert, Elizabeth (2021). *Under a White Sky, The Nature of the Future*. The Bodley Head, London. This is a much more personal account of what to do for nature than her best seller, *The Sixth Extinction*.

21. Krauss, Lawrence M. (2021). *The Physics of Climate Change*. Post Hill Press, New York. This book is a concise discussion of the physical properties that are driving climate change.

22. Lent, Jeremy (2017). *The Patterning Instinct, A Cultural History of Humanity's Search for Meaning*. Prometheus Books. This book supplies an understanding of the importance of patterns in human society and history.

23. Maclean, Norman (2017). *Young Men and Fire*. University of Chicago Press. This is simply the best book describing what it is like to fight a wildfire.

24. Melton, Keith (2005). *Mystic India. An Incredible Journey of Inspiration*. A documentary movie available on Amazon Prime. This video supplies images of celebrations in India.

25. Orner, Eva (2020). *Burning*. This is a film documentary of the black summer of fires in Australia.

26. Progue, David (2021). *How to Prepare for Climate Change, A Practical Guide to Surviving the Chaos*. Simon & Schuster, New York. This book covers personal actions that we can take now. It supplies many of the qualities of arks used in the current story.

27. Riley, Tom (2021). *Born to Storms*. Amazon Books. A Young Adult story that is the first in this arc.

28. Royce, Patrick M. (1988). *Royce's Sailing Illustrated*. Fashion Press. A basic handbook of sailing with a great many graphics and sailing terms explained.

29. Savory, Allen, and Jody Butterfield (2016). *Holistic Management, Third Edition: A Commonsense Revolution to Restore our Environment*. Island Press, London. The basic textbook for growing cattle on marginal land.

30. Simard, Suzanne (2021). *Finding the Mother Tree, Discovering the Wisdom of the Forest*. Alfred A. Knopf, New York. This is a personal guide to understanding how trees work together to become a forest.

31. Snyder, Timothy (2021). *On Tyranny, Graphic Edition*. Ten Speed Press, California. The basic qualities of all authoritarian governments are given. This short book shows why such governments cannot be used to address our climate crisis.

32. St. George, Zach (2020). *The Journeys of Trees, A Story about Forests, People, and the Future*. W. W. Norton & Company, New York. This book provides an understanding of our forests and what we need to do to help them save us.

33. Wadhams, Peter (2017). *A Farewell to Ice: A Report from the Arctic*. Oxford Press, Oxford. This book supplies a deep understanding of what a great loss the end of Arctic ice is.

34. White, Jonathan (2017). *Tides: The Science and Spirit of the Ocean*. Trinity University Press, San Antonio, TX. A book providing an understanding of how our ocean tides work and their effect on human history.

35. Wilson, Edward O. (2017). *Half Earth: Our Planet's Fight for Life*. Liveright Publishing, New York. A book providing a deep understanding of what could be done if half of the land area of Earth is reserved for natural environments. It is by a much beloved author.
Wilson, Edward O. (2012). *The Social Conquest of Earth*. Liveright Publishing, New York. A book providing an understanding of how social animals, from ants to humans, came to predominate on Earth.